Set The Record Straight

Hannah Bonam-Young

Copyright © 2022 by Hannah Bonam-Young

All rights reserved.

The characters and events portrayed in this book are fictitious. Any similarity to real persons, living or dead, is coincidental and not intended by the author.

No part of this book may be reproduced, or stored in a retrieval system, or transmitted in any form or by any means, electronic, mechanical, photocopying, recording, or otherwise, without express written permission of the author.

ISBN-13: 979-8-3645219-5-8

Dear Reader,

I wrote Set The Record Straight to celebrate queer joy around the Holiday season. It is a happy, hopeful, fluffy, sweet read about two women finding love. However, there are some plot points that I felt it best to share before you proceed.

Trigger Warnings: Homophobia, familial estrangement, mentions of religious oppression, and anxiety.

Evan's family kicked her out and have not been in contact since she came out to them at eighteen. They are religious, and use their religion as an excuse for their cruelty. <u>They do not make a reappearance in this book in any capacity. They do not get a redemption arc.</u> However, it is discussed in relation to Evan's feelings, emotions, and memories a few times throughout. Clara's parents are also religious, but are incredibly welcoming of the couple and entirely supportive. <u>There is no homophobia in the story in present happenings.</u>

The reality is that for many of us in the 2SLGTBQIA+ community, the holiday season is difficult. Not all of us can go home. Not all of us can be our full, authentic selves around family. I wanted to write a story that reflected this alongside the hope and fulfillment of finding your own person to build a life and future with.

Lastly, Clara has diagnosed ADHD and Evan is Autistic. As it is in any stories I write, if I do not have direct experience with sensitive subject matter- sensitivity readers are employed to ensure accuracy and positive representation.

Clara and Evan are so special to me. I hope you love them.

Happy Holidays,

SET THE RECORD STRAIGHT

Hannah Bonam-Young

For anyone who was told their love is a sin. It isn't. It's pure magic.

One

Clara

November 15th

The rain ricochets off the sidewalk and raps on my umbrella, the sound like a drumline tapping on a single snare. There's a distant honk, some nearby yelling, splashing of tires. All the sounds that remind me of how much I've missed Toronto. Five months away managed to simultaneously feel like five minutes and five years.

It's bitterly cold today, but not even that can stop the smile on my face or the pep in my step as I walk towards the gallery. I switch the umbrella from one hand to the other, then back again, the anticipatory energy building up in my chest and expanding its way out in movement as it so often does.

I knew while finishing my graduate degree in the spring that Loretta Stole's gallery, DebuTaunt, only hired one new candidate per year. I also knew that they only took applicants in the winter season following a successful fall run. And if it wasn't so successful, they didn't take them at all. But I refused to work anywhere else but for my idol. So I took the risk.

I had some other offers, sure. I impressed my professors, shook the right hands, and got the interviews lined up just in case. I just wanted more. I wanted Loretta—a world-famous, high-concept photographer with an almost forty-year career that I envy.

And while most of my fellow graduates are now shooting weddings for their third Ashley and Brad of the month, reminding kids to remove their fingers from their noses, or posing models in a way that makes their bones sharper, I'm here.

My roommates, Leah and Jen, haven't been shy about admitting they see this gig as a major downgrade, being that it'll be mostly scheduling meetings and coffee runs, but I don't agree. Not at all. Because watching this gallery operate, being a part of that, it's one step closer to having the career I want. Loretta's career, to be exact. And this exact job forty-odd years ago, working for her idol, is how Loretta Stole got her start. That's probably why she has hundreds of applicants every year.

Call it prideful, because it is, but I knew I'd get it. I'm damn good at what I do, and this is what I've been working towards since my seventeenth birthday.

I had come downstairs to a stack of pancakes, a tender note from my mom—who'd left for her shift at the ER already, and a gift sitting next to my father's plate: a neatly tied red ribbon around an emerald green box. My first camera.

I ran outside immediately with it clasped in two fists. Time slowed as I brought it to the apple of my cheek, looked through the lens, and clicked the shutter without a single thought of composition, angle, or perspective.

But even still, I was flooded with pride when I looked at that small playback screen. It was a photo only I could have taken.

Not because of skill, that would come later, but because I was the only one in that exact place at that exact time. The tree was blown by the wind in a way that would never be again. A moment so entirely unique that it would have disappeared forever if not captured by a seventeen-year-old girl and her cheap, entry-level Canon.

Pure magic.

From the second I heard the first click, I was hooked. Enraptured by the idea of collecting unique moments in time. Hoarding stills, poses, and views only I was present for.

I went from Clara, the fairy-sized girl from the middle of nowhere set to attend school for nursing—like her mother and aunts all did—to Clara, the one who constantly had a camera around her neck.

Convincing my parents to let me apply for an undergrad in image arts wasn't as hard as you may expect, considering they were both working-class, no-bullshit folks from farm country. I think they were just happy to see their only child finally passionate about *something*.

For most of my life prior to that point, I'd have considered my parents worried about me. I was one of the rare unicorn little girls who was diagnosed with ADHD early. Mostly because my mother fought every doctor that said I didn't show the classic signs (a.k.a. I didn't have a penis) and won.

The medication kept me pretty listless. The doctors were aiming for me to be more *go with the flow*, but I landed somewhere around *lazy river*. My parents tried all sorts of things. Different motivators, medications, diets. But ultimately, I wasn't a bad kid, and I think they eventually just learned to let me be. I did my homework most of the time, had a few friends, got decent grades, kept a clean room, and didn't really talk back.

But they never stopped encouraging me to find something that ignited a fire in my belly. Like my mom with medicine and my dad with growing crops.

So when they, in perhaps a last-ditch effort, gave me yet *another* hobby that I could hyper-fixate on for a week or two, then quickly drop, I doubt they were expecting it to stick. But it did, and they were thrilled.

My dad came home with a nicer camera three months later. My mom would set up bowls of fruit while packing her work lunch at four a.m., just because it gave me something new to photograph.

And when I turned eighteen, got into the university I wanted, and got *off* those meds—mostly because I kept forgetting to go to the pharmacy—the world opened up. Literally. It felt like I had been wearing 2D glasses at a 3D movie.

Suddenly, my photography got better, I was happier, and—this could be unrelated—I finally got boobs.

Eight years and thirty-thousand dollars in student loans later, here I am. Crossing the street towards the DebuTaunt Gallery. First day as the assistant to Loretta Stole. She was one of my third-year professors during my undergraduate degree, but my obsession with her started far earlier than that. Leah and Jen, who I live with now and *met* in that class, hated me at first. I wouldn't (couldn't) stop listing off Loretta's many accolades to them and anyone else who would listen.

But the jokes on Leah, Jen, and all those other students who called me, often affectionately, a kiss-ass. Because it paid off. I'm here.

I fix the lapel of my beige trench coat, fold and tap my umbrella under the gallery's awning, and take a deep breath. I encapsulate the moment as I normally would with my trusty Lumix-S5, then push open the chic, two-story glass door towards my new beginning.

Two

Evan

I swear to god the moment Remembrance Day is over, the kids only have one thing on their minds. I've helped sew more fucking pom-poms onto red velvet hats today than a real-life elf ever could.

I do love my job. Promise. Before I even attended teacher's college, I knew I wanted to work exclusively with teenagers with learning disabilities. But it's still teaching. Twenty kids with me and occasionally an assistant if I'm lucky, depending on the class list.

However, this year's class is probably my favourite in the past four years. I know I shouldn't say that, but it's the truth. They're a good bunch. They tolerate me, their families are mostly cooperative and engaged, and they've got more entertaining gossip than elderly church ladies at a luncheon. And that's a lot of good gossip. The passive aggressive kind too, which was my personal favourite to eavesdrop on.

Oh, sweet Candice... you know Candice, right? Laura's daughter? Yes, bless her heart. Poor thing has gone and gotten herself knocked up. I know. Heaven bless her. We should keep her and her family in our prayers. Especially the father... whoever he is.

You know... *that*.

This group has those old biddies from my hometown beat. Especially Talia, the firecracker sixteen-year-old who's been in my class now for three years, and her boyfriend, Jacob. They both have Down syndrome, and they're also hands-down the cattiest people I've ever met. I love it. They come to my desk *every day* during their lunch to talk shit about the other students. And they do it loudly too! They don't give a flying fuck who hears them rattling off about how so-and-so totally dyed their hair because so-and-so did first or how Logan has a crush on Serena, but Serena likes Keisha, and henceforth.

I have to attempt to be professional and shut down the conversations most days, but it's truly one of the best parts of the job.

Though I can't help but wonder whether the gossip mongers of Augustine High School know about Natalie and me. They certainly knew we were dating. One of the students caught a glimpse of my background screen once while I was googling something for him. He made sure everyone knew that Ms. Paul and Ms. Callway were "hooking up" based on the photo of us cuddling on the beach.

Then they noticed when I started wearing my engagement ring this past spring. They *loudly* noticed. They *enthusiastically* noticed. And every single one of them had passed around and tried on my beautiful oval solitaire.

But there have been no comments since I took it off and returned it to Natalie in September.

I should have guessed they'd let me be. One of the many cool things about working alongside kids with disabilities is unlearning years of false assumptions. So often they're being judged, pitied, or granted condescending sympathy by the masses. But in reality, they're the ones who know when to talk shit and when to mind their business. When someone's hurting and needs an extra-long hug. When to joke and when not to. Part of the reason I finally decided to get my formal autism diagnosis was because of these kids. They taught me to shed the shame of being *different*. They have the gift of true emotional intelligence, and I'm grateful for them.

Especially lately, because it's been a rough couple of months.

Natalie and I weren't happy for a long time. I can see that now. I felt a slow shift, sure. But what I mistook for settling in, Natalie had quietly labelled settling. What I believed to be comfortable silence, Natalie thought unbearable.

I know I played a part in that. I'm not the most affectionate person. Not the most romantic, naturally. I can get easily overwhelmed, overcrowded, overstimulated. However, I do wish Natalie hadn't tried to spice things up by proposing—as she admitted when loading the last box into her truck—and maybe just *talked* to me.

I also wish that truck wasn't driving straight to Lisa's house... or Ms. Turner, shall I call her. It's always the history teachers. The horny fuckers. You'd think they'd know what happens to people who cheat on their partners. Anne Boleyn, anyone?

Now I'm sure students catch glimpses of Natalie's lock screen, which is presumably a photo of her and Lisa together, and know some shit went down. Teenagers can be cruel, sure, but this group is merciful. And they're about the only things that have helped me trudge through these last few months.

My lock screen is now my cat, Bagel. (He's bread-coloured beige with black and grey spots like poppy seeds, and I was *really* hungry when I went to the shelter—you cannot blame me.)

Did I adopt a cat the very day after my fiancée left me? Why thank you so much for asking. Yes, I did. Do I regret it? A fair amount, actually, yes. Bagel likes to sandwich himself (ironically) between the wall and the back of my fridge. He gets stuck and then screams until I come home. My neighbours even called the cops once because they thought I was hurting him.

That was a new low. I'd hoped from my upturned nods and grimacing smiles in passing that my neighbours would have gathered I'm not a cat-murderer. But I have been told I have an extraordinarily intense resting bitch face, so maybe they presumed the worst.

I was voted "least approachable" in my high school yearbook, which I still believe hadn't been a category the year prior. I've had only a small handful of real friends my entire life, and they're all from my hometown, and I haven't been back in a long, long time now.

One of these friends though, Clara, has recently moved to the city. Well, moved back, I suppose. She was in Toronto for university too, but I'd been so wrapped up in Natalie since the beginning of teacher's college that I didn't really have time for friends beyond her.

Plus, Clara has been busy too, finishing her undergrad and master's degree—making a name for herself in the photography world.

It's not that we had a falling out or ever decided to not be best friends anymore. It's just that we've been close since we were nine, so it's easy to sort of *forget* about each other until we need a familiar face. Fading in and out of each other's lives like the lingering silence between songs—just a lull, not an end. And lately, we've been talking more again.

She's just landed a new job at a gallery, and it's a really big deal to her. Her eyes went as wide as saucers when she described this place over a video call last week. She was in her childhood bedroom at Daryl and Maggie's house, packing up boxes. I was in bed, eating Thai food with *The Bachelorette* on mute.

Clara often needs someone to call her when she's completing a task—to just keep her mind off other things while she finishes what she set out to do—which has been great. Not only to catch up, but because the nights have been really fucking lonely since Natalie left.

Tonight I'm taking her out to my favourite local spot to celebrate her first day. We haven't actually hung out in person since... God, I don't even remember. Definitely before I finished school, but I can't recall a time after that.

Clara is adamant this dinner is also a toast to my newfound singleness. And that she, despite being straight, would make a fantastic wingwoman to an unapproachable lesbian like myself. But that's not happening. I'll probably die alone, alongside Bagel's great-granddaughter, who will eat my face before my neighbours (who were much more eager to call before) let the police know about a weird smell and find my body.

It's not that I'm some Frankenstein-looking monster. I've been hit on occasionally. Women at bars will tell me I look *just like that girl from* New Girl, and I tell them that her name is Zooey Deschanel and that she gave her daughter the middle name Otter. Otter! Who does that?

That sort of kills the conversation each time. Ergo, it seems to be my personality that will keep me in perpetual singledom. Natalie was my first real love, and I let that fade off and die, *entirely* unaware. If I couldn't keep a peppy, well-to-do mathematics teacher from losing interest and cheating on me, there's probably zero hope for anyone else to stick around long term.

The closest thing to love I think I'll ever get again is reality TV, which is actually a not-so-guilty pleasure of mine. A therapist may use the term *special interest.*

Regardless, I'm fascinated by how those beautiful idiots can fall in love stepping out of a limo, through a wall, or on an island. Though I suppose that last one isn't exactly a hardship. Paradise, away from the real world and the realities of life, would probably make love easy to do.

I could go for that. Four weeks on an island... a bunch of hot people doing hot people stuff. However, my five-foot-eight averagely un-exercised body, self-induced crisis curtain bangs, and wide-framed glasses don't *exactly* make me their ideal candidate. I'm fairly certain all of those women have at least six pairs of matching bra and underwear sets in all the same (and properly fitting) sizes. They also all have gym memberships and pay to have their teeth whitened and hair highlighted.

All power to them. They look incredible, and I love to watch. That's just not me.

Clara could be on a show like that, actually. She has a petite, toned frame and perfectly styled blond hair. Nice teeth too. The prettiest eyes I think I've ever seen. The twinkling kind, like she's constantly wowed by everything around her.

Oop. Been a while since I had to remind myself not to think about Clara *that* way. Or straight women in general, really. No, we haven't pulled *that* familiar reminder out since college around the "bi-curious" girls who are often "bi... for their boyfriends who watched a certain type of porn and wanted to see their girlfriend make out with me."

For a while—and by a *while*, I mean seven troublesome years of my adolescence—Clara was my best friend most of the time and, sometimes consecutively, my unachievable dream girl. I'd like to chalk it up to the fact that it was a small town, that she was my closest friend, and that my little-baby-queer heart didn't have many options, but that'd be a lie. Clara was special. *Is* special. She's a mosaic of a person. So many differing, unique elements that create one perfect thing. A little chaotic and a whole lot of mess involved—but beautiful all the same.

But that doesn't change the fact that she's not interested in women. Sure, maybe a teeny lingering of a crush will always remain—because it was my first—but that's all it'll ever be, and I'm completely fine with it. Our friendship is incredibly important to me. For many reasons, but one being that Clara's my last remaining piece of home.

And with that sobering thought, I get a pom-pom to the face thrown by Talia.

"Ms. Paul, focus up!" she berates me.

I grumble, reaching for my needle and thread. "Don't throw things."

"Watch how you talk to my girlfriend," Jacob pipes up.

I shut him down with a withering stare. "Cool it, loverboy. This is still my classroom."

Three

Clara

So, honestly, my first day isn't going the way I expected it to. For starters, I don't have a desk. I have a clipboard with a pen on a string and a belt clip for a phone. Apparently, Loretta likes to be *able to move where the moment takes her*, and *desks keep creativity sitting*. I should have worn more comfortable shoes.

Everyone who works here is dressed like they just left a very chic funeral where they may or may not have been responsible for the wealthy deceased's life coming to an untimely end. All black, all designer, all intimidating.

I'm in a brown plaid suit jacket that I thrifted and had my roommate Jen tailor to fit me, an emerald green blouse, and ripped jeans. This shit was *the look* in my graduate program. Professional aloof. I've apparently missed the trends change since leaving Toronto for five months, and now the look is rich, gothic vampire.

I'll have to go shopping.

Loretta has been pacing back and forth in an entirely glass-panelled meeting room above the main gallery space for three hours. It looks out over the exhibition below and is the only enclosed room I've yet to see. She's alone with nothing in her hands or on her person, except for the matches and cigarette she pulled out of her pocket at one point—which may have actually been a joint based on the faint smell wafting around the hallway.

I was simply instructed to wait for her to exit the room by the previous year's assistant-turned-guest-gallerist, Heather. She told me sternly that under no circumstances am I allowed to go in. If the phone rings, answer it. Two words only. *Hello. DebuTaunt.* That's it.

"We do not ask how people are. We do not ask the reason for their call. We don't waste time," Heather said, picking lint off *my* shoulder.

I nodded and asked where the staff bathroom was. She pointed with a limp wrist, not looking up from her phone. I've still not found it, and honestly, I'll probably never ask again. I may be in over my head here. Just as I'm about to do a lap to see if I can spot a door that vaguely resembles a bathroom entrance, Loretta stills.

Like *completely* stills. As if some grand maestro held his conductor's baton in midair as she was halfway through another step back towards the opposite wall.

She then swiftly exits the room, throwing the door open like she doesn't know her own strength. I take a step back and almost fall as she approaches me. Loretta's six-foot wafer-thin frame floats towards me with black fabric ribbons off her dress drifting behind her like ink in water.

"Clara." She stops closer to me than I'd have expected. The corners of her eyes are wrinkled with age and affection. I breathe for the first time in at least a full minute.

"Hi, Loretta. Hi. It's such a pleasure to—"

"You were chosen, Clara," she says, interrupting me. "Own that. No more thank-yous or platitudes. We're colleagues now, dear." She rolls up the sleeves of her dress, revealing the dark brown skin of her forearms, frail and thin, then pats her chin with a curled index finger. "You were the one with the obituary exhibition, yes?"

"Y-y-yes," I stutter, then clear my throat. "Yes, I was." My senior thesis right before graduation was shown in the Museum of Contemporary Art not far from here. Six photographs in which I played with light and old film reels to meld together the model's haunted expressions with the photo they thought would be used at their funeral if they'd suddenly passed.

"It was excellent."

I'm sweating. I can feel it pooling above my upper lip. "Thank you."

She raises a brow in warning, but I ponder what I'm supposed to say if *not* thank you. *I know* is arrogant... "It performed well," is what I come up with. Pretentious as hell, but alas.

"Truthfully, with all the attention the exhibition received, I didn't expect you to apply for this position."

This answer I've prepared for. "I wanted to start at DebuTaunt because I truly believe it to be the best gallery Toronto has to offer. Being here and assisting you will help me become a more well-rounded artist."

"In what sense?" Loretta leans back, crossing her arms. I take a moment to realise that we're in the hallway, and I may be a lot more comfortable sitting at a desk right now in a private office where my new co-workers couldn't hear me totally fawning.

"I admire your career. The legacy you've built. I believe I need a stronger business sense and an understanding of management in order to—"

"To be me." She sighs.

I'm losing her. "No," I say defensively, to which she cocks her head. *Shit. Speak*! "When I found photography, I felt like a shell of a person." Oh god, word vomit. "The moment I picked up a camera, I found myself. Respectfully, Loretta, I don't want to be you. I want to have the career you've had. I want to be as successful as you. I want to be respected for my art like you. When I saw your 2012 collection for the Canadian Museum of Contemporary Photography in Ottawa—it *changed* me. I want to change people. But that doesn't come from just being a damn good photographer. There are things I can't learn without watching firsthand."

She blinks, fluttering her eyelids elegantly. And I didn't expect it. Her indifferent, perhaps bothered, expression softened to something so sincere. A twitch of her lips into a demure smile. A depth to her eyes previously missing. I'm getting through to her. She's seeing me now, and it's fucking exhilarating.

"That was my favourite collection," she says, every word drawn out. "It's not one that's often talked about."

I involuntarily shake my head. "That's such a shame."

"Well…" She taps her elbow, studying me. "You know how this world can be."

I nod. I think she's insinuating that it didn't receive the same public attention or accolades because it was a presentation mostly focused on the queer experience. Most of the photographs were obscenely vulnerable. Levels of varying naked models in positions that evoked lust, horror, pride, sadness, joy. It was only a decade ago, but even then, it was slightly taboo for the museum to host such a provocative collection.

"Clara…" She takes my left hand in hers, admires my lavender-stone ring that belonged to my grandmother, and smiles to herself. "It is not easy to be a woman in this field. It is not easy to carve a spot for yourself in a mountain when your male colleagues have chisels and jackhammers, whereas you have nothing but your fingernails." She pats my wrist before lowering my hand.

I nod like she's the preacher in the pulpit at the front of my parents' congregation. I damn near say *amen*.

"But it's even harder for us."

Wait, what?

"When men cannot obtain you, they are far less likely to promote you. Remember that."

Oh, she thinks I'm engaged. Maybe? I fiddle with my grandmother's ring and stutter something that sounds like "sorry" as she opens her burgundy-painted lips to speak again.

"I am very intentional about who I hire at this gallery. Who I promote and show. This is a very *intentional* space."

I nod. I know that. She only shows the best of the best here. But why is she—

The phone on my hip begins ringing.

"Answer that. I'm supposed to be in a meeting right now anyway. Laurence will be in shortly. He'll take you under his wing." She stops me from reaching for the phone's holster.

"Thank you for being so candid with me, Clara." Then she's drifting away, silk chiffon tendrils following after her.

And I'm very fucking confused as I hit the call button and say, "Thank you for calling DebuTaunt. This is Clara speaking," and watch as Heather grinds her teeth together from the far side of the hallway.

Fuck.

Four

Evan

"Clara... she thinks you're gay," I say for the third time, looking at my sweet, naive friend across the booth from me.

She mumbles her disagreement into her martini and licks her lips after, her throat bobbing. "No." She swallows again. "No way." She fiddles with the olive in her glass. "People aren't that presumptuous."

"Clara, you complimented a *gay* icon on her most obscure gallery collection about *gay* culture that she put on *during* pride month. She told you it's harder for women like *you*." I lean across the table slightly, raising my eyebrows. "She thinks you're gay."

She pulls her full bottom lip between her teeth, wincing. "Shit."

"Just correct her. It's fine."

She reaches for her drink and tilts her head back, eyes tightening as she gulps every last sip. A laugh escapes me, perhaps a little at her expense. "It's not a big deal," I tell her.

"No, it is. I didn't know what it seemed like and... that's not where the story ends."

I fight a teasing smirk. Clara and I have been friends for almost two decades, and we've been through a lot together. It's great to have friends that you can just dive back into life with. No bullshit. No small talk. None of the shit that makes my brain feel jammed like a phone's busy signal.

And our relationship has always sort of existed in a teasing, silly way. We get a little hyper together and more sarcastic than I let myself be with other people. Because if Clara interprets something differently than I intended it, she just asks. She's not one to let anything fester. Almost as if every thought or question of hers has to get *out* to make room for more. So I can relax a little knowing that I won't upset her. And if I do, she'll let me know.

"What did you do?" I ask, voice smug.

"We were in a budget meeting at the end of the day. Everyone was just making polite chit-chat and—" Clara picks up the small paper menu and covers half her face.

"Clara." I elongate her name, half laughing. "Come on, it can't be that bad."

"I said I was going out for dinner with my girlfriend tonight. To celebrate the first day on the job."

I genuinely try to fight it, I do, but a snort-like laugh escapes through my nose.

"No!" she whines, reaching for a now empty glass. I take that as my cue and walk to the bar to order another round.

From here, I can see Clara biting her fingernails between running her hands through her hair. It's far longer than she had it last spring when I saw her on the subway. Though she got off before I said anything.

I'm not sure why, but seeing her out of context like that, unexpectedly—it caught me off guard. Honestly, before I realised it was Clara, I had been checking out the beautiful blond stranger nodding along to whatever was playing from their headphones. She was wearing these black ripped jeans and army boots that I loved. I remember thinking her ass looked fantastic, especially as she softly swayed to the music only she could hear. Then she turned. And I froze momentarily before averting my eyes.

She is still as beautiful now as she always has been.

And she really does give off... *vibes*, though obviously unintentionally. My lifelong friend has described herself as "tragically straight" when asked. While teenage me believed that to *truly* be a tragedy, I'm far past that crush now. *Far past it.*

The bartender slides a martini and my glass of merlot across the bar, so I make my way back towards Clara, who looks so agitated she may burst out of her skin.

"It's going to be fine," I say, setting down her drink.

The words are barely out before she's already taking a large gulp and hissing at the first taste.

"I didn't really think about it before, Ev, but... they're all gay. Everyone I worked with today mentioned their partners, and Loretta said this thing about being intentional about who she hires. Do I..." She licks her lips, then her brow furrows as she looks at the table between us. "Do I give off a certain... vibe?"

"Yes." I don't hesitate. "Sort of." I try to soften the answer.

"Right." She nods. "I mean, other people have told me that before."

"Natalie thought you were," I tell her, finishing a languishing sip of wine. "She was always trying to set you up with a friend of ours."

Natalie and Clara only met once. I was in my last year of teacher's college, and Nat threw me a party for my twenty-fifth. They seemed to get along fine *at* the party. But afterwards, Nat turned rather interrogatory about Clara. I remember, despite being rather tipsy, having to tell her multiple times that Clara wasn't interested in women. But that's when Nat hit me with a question I didn't expect: "Yeah, but are *you* interested in *her*?" she had spat.

I didn't answer. Couldn't. Hypothetical questions are *always* a bad idea.

"Oh my god!" Clara exclaims, bringing my attention back to the dimly lit restaurant.

I look over my shoulder, as if there must be a shocking revelation behind me causing Clara to speak so abruptly and loudly.

"Oh my god," she mutters, putting her face in her hands.

"What?" I ask incredulously.

"I'm a fucking idiot, Ev."

"Explain," I demand, reaching for another sip of wine and pushing my glasses up my nose.

"Loretta told me to bring my girlfriend to the gallery opening, and I said I would."

Sweet summer child. "Okay..." I shrug. "You just need to explain you don't have a girlfriend and move on."

"So they think I'm an idiot? Or worse, a liar? A gay fraud? A gaud!"

I tilt my head, weighing the options. "It's just a simple misunderstanding."

"No, it's not. It was first day nerves mixed with an inability to focus on one moment and think about the bigger picture, and shit—I've ruined it."

"You haven't ruined anything," I argue.

"I have! What if they only hired me because I'm gay?"

"You're not gay."

"Exactly!"

"Are you seriously claiming reverse discrimination? In this year of our Lord two thousand and twenty-two?" I tease, smiling into my wineglass.

"No? No," she asks, then answers herself immediately. "Well…"

"Clara," I chastise, smiling ear to ear.

"I think that's an amazing thing! I think that if Loretta wants to exclusively work with artists who are gay, then that's what she should do. I think that's fine!"

"Well, so long as *you* think it's fine."

She glares affectionately, a laugh breaking through. "Fuck off."

"So what are you going to do?" I ask.

Clara places her cheek on the table, and I grimace, wondering when it was properly sanitised last. "I guess I have two choices. Come clean and look like a complete dunce to the one person I've been wanting to impress for almost a decade or…"

"Or?" I ask.

"Be gay?"

"So it's a choice? Wow, the congregation back home will be delighted to hear you've changed your stance," I quip.

Clara's face falls immediately. I swallow wine. *You've made her uncomfortable.*

"When was the last time you went home?" she asks solemnly.

"Haven't been back since we left. Ten years," I answer coldly. I started dating Natalie only a year after leaving home, making it much easier to forget about my family.

Nat's family was warm and welcoming and incredibly supportive of their daughter. We went there for every holiday. They sent cards for birthdays and notes for no reason and checked in often. When Nat and I got engaged, her mom offered to dance with me while Natalie danced with her dad at the reception. That meant a lot to me.

But ultimately, I wasn't their kid. So when Nat left, they sent one last message wishing me well, and that was it. The end of a nine-year relationship, and truly I'm not sure who I'm most upset about losing.

"I'm sorry." Clara sighs, reaching across the table and holding my hand in hers. "I hate that."

"I know." I slide my hand free and scratch my chin. I hadn't really considered just how difficult this holiday season would be until this afternoon, and not just because it'll be my first alone in a decade. It was the small red envelope I found in my staff room cubby this afternoon.

Augustine's staff holiday party. December tenth. This year's hosts? None other than my ex and the fucking history teacher. At the home they now live in. Together. With a fucking dog, according to social media. Natalie hates dogs.

But Natalie hated a lot of things she now tolerates. Like hosting work events and people who cheat on their partners. None of it makes sense.

"I have an idea." The words tumble out of me. "I think I have a solution that will help us both," I add before taking a *hefty* sip of liquid courage.

Five

Clara

"They're hosting the fucking Christmas party?" I yell, then quickly apologise to the people in the booth behind me. "They're hosting the fucking Christmas party?" I ask again, whispering angrily.

Evan nods, finishing her glass of red wine that matches her lipstick colour near perfectly. I should ask her where she got it. The shade makes her lips look like a crisp apple. *Focus, Clara.*

"Those assholes." My nostrils flare. "Flaunting isn't even the right word for it. That's downright cruel."

"I feel like I must have done something to really piss her off."

"What? No way. You're the nicest person that's ever lived," I say.

Evan scoffs, so I fight back. "Seriously! For example, you just let me rant about my problem—that *I caused*—for over an hour while you were sitting on the holiday party invite from hell."

"Right. So... back to that." Evan pushes her glasses up her thin nose, and I notice the bump she has there from tobogganing when we were teenagers. I steered us left when I should have gone right. She got whacked in the face with a branch so hard it split her glasses in two and broke her nose. I wonder if I ever apologised for that properly. I should do that.

"Hey, I'm sorry—"

"We should date," Evan says at the same time.

"What?" I blink rapidly.

"Not like that... You have to bring a girlfriend to this gallery opening, right? To not look like a... *gaud*? And I have to attend a holiday party at my ex-fiancée's house that she shares with her current partner in front of all of our colleagues, who know some shit went down. It's humiliating."

"Okay..." I wait for Evan to continue, my mind whirling. That *could* be from the two martinis though.

"Let's just be each other's dates. I'll be your fake girlfriend, and you be mine. Two nights—that's it."

I purse my lips. "But Natalie knows I'm straight," I counter. "She'll see right through it."

"Except," Evan's smile is devilish, "she always thought you weren't. She loves being right more than she'd want to have the upper hand relationship-wise. She'll be pissed because she always suspected it, and the minute she left me—"

"I swooped in," I gasp. "How scandalous of me! I was just waiting on the sidelines for you to be single."

"Exactly." Evan giggles, and I count that as a win. Getting full laughs out of Ev has been difficult for as long as I can remember. "It's the perfect plan."

A slow creeping smile appears on my face as I consider the plan. "In a few months, I'll just pretend to be really sad and say we broke up." I cross my arms, tapping my bicep as thoughts rush in and through me. "It really is a great plan, Ev. But..." I don't finish my thought, distracted by my internal debate.

"Then, when or if you're with a guy and want to bring him to a gallery event—hey, you're bi."

"Yeah, sexuality is fluid! Things change." I nod faster and faster. "This might be a great idea."

"Thank you. I have them occasionally." Evan's crooked smile grows.

"But... it wouldn't be weird? I mean, to pretend?"

Evan shrugs. "I don't think so."

"No?" I ask.

"We could make rules." She dabs her lip with a napkin, some of the lipstick leaving a stain. I really do need to ask where she got that. It's gorgeous.

First, ask about rules. "Such as?"

"No kissing."

"Ah, yes."

"Minimal PDA," Evan offers, shrugging.

I tut. "Not sure about that one. You know me. I'm a very touchy, tactile person. It would seem suspicious."

Evan nods, looking off to the side as a party of people filters into the restaurant loudly. "That's true. Okay, um, just no kissing then? That's the only rule?"

"I mean..." I laugh and Evan rolls her eyes. "A little peck here and there might help sell it." I grin mischievously.

"I'm having flashbacks to college." Evan shudders. "Are you experimenting with me, Teens?"

Wow, it's been a very long time since anyone called me that other than my parents. Teens, short for Teeny, for obvious reasons. It brings up a melancholy, nostalgic feeling that somehow falters into a contented smile. "I wouldn't use you like that, Evan." The words come out far more serious than I intended, but I do want her to know that.

I pour both of us more water as the waiter begins walking towards us with our main courses. "But who knows? Maybe I'm a late bloomer." I wink, adding the levity I was briefly missing.

Then, once our food is settled in front of us, a question forms I can't seem to shake off. "How *did* you know?"

"That I like women?" Evan clarifies, and I nod. "Um... I guess I just heard friends talk about boys in the way I realised I only felt about girls. And it was a slow realisation, obviously. I didn't even know lesbians existed until I was twelve and watched *Ellen* after school. The only thing I knew about gay people was from church—and it was ugly. But honestly, I thought that was just men."

I nod. "I thought that too. I remember seeing two women together at a grocery store once with my mom when I was like... eleven? And being really confused."

Evan nods, smiling softly. "Did you ask Maggie about them?"

"Yeah." I laugh, take a quick sip, and roll my eyes with affection. "She told me they were in love, to mind my business, and go fetch a three-pound bag of russets."

I watch Evan's expression turn from amused to distracted, eyes glazing over and lips tugging downward. I want to ask more questions about her coming out experience, but I don't want to pry. She's not a closed-off person. More like a cavern you can only explore on low tide.

"Can I ask you something?" Evan blinks, coming back into the room from whatever memory she followed.

"Of course," I answer.

"When did you first think that maybe I was different?"

I bite down a smile. "You used to make my Barbies kiss."

"No I did not!" Evan bursts, her cheeks turning as red as her lips.

"You did. Plus, you noticed things I never really did. I remember you saying—we were probably, like, thirteen—that kissing a man would be awful because of facial hair. It made me think, *well, then you should just kiss girls.* And I remember it sort of being an unspoken thing after that. Until—"

"My eighteenth birthday."

"Yeah," I agree.

Evan came out to her very religious parents on her eighteenth birthday. We've only talked about it once, the same day it occurred, when she came to my house. My mom answered the door, and she immediately broke down crying on our front porch. It was just a week after Christmas, and she was literally thrown out in the cold by them.

I had never seen her cry before. Hadn't really even seen her get close in the nine years up till that point. Not at church—when everyone else would be crying, supposedly moved by the holy spirit—not when her beloved dog passed away, or when her older sister got into a bad car accident. But she cried then. And, though I wish I could say differently, it freaked me out. I sat on the bottom step of our kitchen stairs as my mom sat her down at the table, got her some tea, and had her explain what happened.

It only took my mom thirty seconds to say she could stay with us. Not many more to send my dad with his truck over there to pick up her things—which had already been tossed into a snow mound.

I watch as Evan unwraps her cutlery and twirls it between her thumb and finger, then sets it down beside her plate, her expression far more serious than I've seen tonight. "Natalie really blindsided me..." She looks up hesitantly, softly finding my eyeline. "Is it bad that I want her to hurt like I did? Just a little?"

I ponder the question because I don't have to lie to Evan—never have. "I don't think so." I sigh, reflecting some more. "I think that's only human. What she did was really, really wrong."

"And you don't mind being a part of that?"

I shake my head, our eye contact fusing across the table. Her dark brown and my blue holding space for each other silently. "No," I answer plainly. Something like protectiveness rises in my chest over my kind friend who's been through so much already. Too much. "No, I'd key her car if you asked. I'd go full Carrie Underwood. A Louisville slugger to both headlights."

"Not the full Carrie," Evan mutters, digging into her risotto and smiling to herself.

"I'd make Carrie look tame for you, Ev." I wink, shovelling a forkful of lasagna into my mouth.

Six

Evan

November 29th

It's been two weeks since Clara and I made our plan that she's dubbed Operation Merry and Gay. It was either that or Ho-Ho-Homo. I think I chose the lesser of two evils. Though both made me smile.

I like that she says every thought that pops into her head. Occasionally she'll wince after, like she's perhaps said the wrong thing, but honestly, I find it endearing. Even if it's not always the *most* socially acceptable. She's got a good heart. Her whole family does.

We've been texting a lot but haven't met up since her first day at the new job. The gallery has her working a lot of evenings, and (strange, I know) teaching mostly happens during school hours.

Clara's usually just starting her day when I'm eating lunch. I take my break at a different time than the rest of the staff. High school kids require little supervision over lunch for the most part. A simple rotation of hall monitors and cafeteria watch does them fine. But my kids need someone with them at all times, so I switch off with another teacher and take my lunch earlier than most.

It's quiet. I like that.

Enjoying a turkey and provolone in the pleasure of my own company is truly one of my favourite things. The staff room has been decorated for the season. It's charming. In a Buddy the Elf went overboard sort of way. The art teachers are most likely responsible for the twinkling lights, dozens of hanging craft-paper stars, and chain-link bunting overhead.

I'm just noticing a snag that will give way to a full tear in my tights under the burgundy dress I'm wearing when voices approach down the hall in the offices. I take a bite of my sandwich and position myself for ideal eavesdropping. Then immediately regret it.

Giggling. Familiar giggling. Natalie's. And another voice I recognize shushing her flirtatiously. Lisa's.

God, if you're real like my mother insists you are, please don't let them come in here. Lock the door. Start a fire. Strike me dead. Anything.

"So did *she* RSVP?" Lisa asks Natalie right outside the door. I know by the way she said it, *she* means *me*. Bile starts climbing up my throat, and suddenly, turkey and provolone is entirely unappetizing.

"Yeah." I hear a breathless rasp that resembles a faint laugh. "With a plus one."

"No!" Lisa finds this *hilarious*.

"Mm-hmm..." One of them rattles the door handle, and I pray to disappear. Time slows, and before I think, I'm reaching into my bag on the table for my phone. I hit Clara's name and *Call* so quickly I swear I've broken the speed of light.

"Ev? You okay?" A huskier version of Clara answers that has my mouth turning dry. Is that what she sounds like when she wakes up? It's intoxicating.

"Hey, you," I say, just as Natalie and Lisa turn the corner and spot me. "I'm sorry, beautiful. Did I wake you?"

A contented, sleepy sigh meets me and does fuzzy things to my brain. "Yes, but I love waking up to your voice."

I'll give it to her. Clara is quick on her feet. She probably thinks she's on speaker. I don't tell her otherwise... *yet.*

"I'm just having lunch and missed you." I hold my phone by pressing it between my shoulder and ear and pick at the chipped black polish on my right hand in order to stop myself from looking towards Nat and Lisa. The two of them are still lingering behind me at the coffee machine, probably exchanging *that was close* expressions. "How are you feeling?"

"You mean after last night?" Clara giggles. "Baby," she purrs. "I'm still—"

"No, you're not on speaker." I wince, crossing and uncrossing my legs under the table. "Sorry, I should have said."

"Oh, okay." She laughs. "Who's around? Natalie?"

"Yeah."

I hear a shuffling of sheets and a soft groan that to me sounds like Clara sitting up in bed. I imagine the wild, loose bun on top of her head that she used to get after our sleepovers growing up.

My heart blooms a little at the thought. "Okay, repeat after me," she says calmly.

I can feel my cheeks flushing, a woozy sort of rush as I say, "okay," and chew at my thumbnail.

"I know. I can't wait either," she says in a *slow,* sultry voice I've never heard from her before. Then I repeat, less effectively, I'm sure, because speaking suddenly seems very difficult.

"Oh is *that* what you have planned...?" She giggles so delicately the hairs on the back of my neck stand up. I do my best to mimic her, exactly as I can.

"Now ask me what I'm wearing."

"Clara, I can't. I'm at work." I laugh, breathless.

"See, that's much more natural. Perfect. That'll have Nat guessing." Clara's pride is audible.

I clear my throat. "Can I see you later?" I ask.

"For real or?"

"Yes. I'll stop by the gallery?" Step one of the operation—a casual drop-by at Clara's work.

"Okay," Clara answers definitively. "I'll pretend to forget my dinner at home. Can you come by the gallery with some takeout? I'll introduce you to a few people."

"Sushi?"

"Definitely that, but what was Natalie's favourite place?"

"Thai? From Sahla?"

"Mmm. Absolutely not." Clara laughs. "But do you think she heard?"

I look at the buckle on my knee-high leather boots and reach down, pretending to adjust it as I peek over my shoulder. Lisa is getting creamer out of the fridge as Natalie just stands rigidly in front of the kitchenette's counter.

"I think so."

"Okay. Big finish... ready?"

"Yeah." I take a sip from my emotional support water bottle.

"I'll see you later, honey. Love you."

"I'll see you later, honey," I respond flatly.

"Wow, rude!" Clara exclaims.

I can't help but laugh.

"C'mon say it."

"You too. Bye."

Clara's mid-complaint when I hang up and tuck my phone into my bag. I sit straight in my chair, keeping my eyes focused on the wall in front of me until Natalie finally leaves, Lisa trailing after her.

Seven

Clara

I make my way to the apartment's kitchen and find Jen yelling at the blender.

"God dammit!" She hits the top of it four times in a row, groaning out profanities. "This fucking thing never fucking works!" she yells over her shoulder at me.

I politely step around her, grab the cord, and plug it in. It starts instantly.

"Oh." Her entire demeanour changes. Suddenly a beaming ray of sunshine.

"Morning."

"More like midday." She pats my head like a puppy. "Work late?"

"Yeah. The printer sent the gallery's invites uncut, and it was too late to return them. So it was me and a paper trimmer up until almost three in the morning. I'm lucky I kept all my fingers intact."

"Still enjoying it?" Jen asks me, pouring her smoothie into a tall glass.

"Yes. Being around Loretta has already taught me so much. I don't think it's too presumptuous to think that by this time next year, I'll be in Heather's shoes, debuting my own show."

"And what about the... what was it again? Jingle all the gay?" She takes a long sip.

I giggle. "No, but that's a good one too. Operation Merry and Gay."

"How's that going?"

"Just got off the phone with Ev. Her ex was around, and we had a flirty little chat." I waggle my eyebrows and reach above Jen's head for a mug. "She's going to stop by the gallery later today with dinner. Do the rounds with my co-workers."

Jen's eyes turn judgy and cold as she slurps back more smoothie.

I glare right back playfully until she softens. "It's really not that bad of an idea." Jen and Leah both made their thoughts on the plan perfectly clear when I announced the arrangement to them the morning after it was decided upon. I believe Leah said something along the lines of, *this is the stupidest thing I've ever heard.*

"You should just come shoot weddings with me. The money is good, and you don't have to lie to everyone to do it." She flourishes with a long, judgy sip.

"I love how much you enjoy it, Jen, but that's just not what I want to do."

"She wants to be Loretta Stole!" Leah shouts from the living room, apparently back from running errands. She drops two grocery bags onto the dining table, picks some items out, and then comes towards the fridge to slot a few green juices inside. "Plus, maybe she isn't lying. Perhaps our dear Clara is realising she wants a taste of Evan's goodies."

Both Jen and I groan.

Leah stands straight, aghast. "Oh please. I'm just saying once you try pus—"

"What Leah is trying to say, indelicately," Jen raises her hand to shush Leah, "is that maybe don't knock it until you try it?"

"Have you? Tried it?" Leah asks me, arms crossed. "Considered it?"

"Because it's not like you're ever bringing guys around either," Jen adds matter-of-factly.

I shrug, pouring myself coffee from the pot. Leah hands me the creamer without having to ask, then shuts the door with her hip. "You know me. I'm just not... all that interested in romance. I've had a one-track mind for a decade. Finish school, work for Loretta, be the next great photographer. I follow the plan."

I raise my mug to take a sip and hopefully end this conversation when Leah comes out swinging. "Are you a virgin?"

I damn near do a spit take. "No." I choke. "No, thanks for checking."

"Did you... enjoy it?" Jen asks hesitantly.

"I mean, I guess?" I wince. "It was fine."

"I, for one, love when my sexual partners describe our love-making as *fine*." Jen shakes her head, laughing softly to herself.

"I was in my head the whole time! Wondering what he was thinking about, how I looked, how I felt to him, if I was doing it right, if I'd locked my door, if I should pretend to finish, if—"

"Dear god," Leah whispers.

"Is that... bad?"

"No," Jen says firmly. "No, of course not."

"Can I ask you something?" Leah leans back on the counter, crossing one leg around the other. I wave her on. "When you're walking down the street—do you check people out? Do you ever think to yourself, *wow, I'd love to kiss them* or...?"

My eyes roll upwards and to the left as I begin searching my memories. I've definitely thought about people's clothes or noticed when someone would make an incredible model for work, but I've never wanted to kiss a stranger. Honestly, the idea of that is a little repulsive. "Not really. Do most people do that?"

"Not everyone..." Leah's features soften. "But it could mean you're demisexual."

"Remind me?" I ask.

"People who are demisexual typically only form a sexual attraction to a person once they have formed a close emotional bond with them."

"Oh." That does *sound* like me. "Huh."

"Have you ever had sex with someone you had an established relationship or bond with?" she asks.

"No, not really. After a few dates, it felt sort of... obligatory? Not in a bad way. Just, no."

"And you and Evan... you've known each other since forever, right?"

"Since we were nine, yeah." *Oh.* "But I don't really feel that with her. Like, I don't want to rip her clothes off either."

"So maybe you *are* straight but need that connection first." Jen shrugs, smiling politely.

"Yeah, maybe." I take a languishing sip of warm coffee, feeling it soothe my throat and settle in my stomach. "I just think maybe I'm not a sexual person. I honestly could go without it just fine."

"Which is a cruel irony because you're insanely hot." Jen and Leah high-five in agreement, and I can't help but laugh alongside them.

"Well, ladies, it's been lovely chatting, but I better be off. Engagement shoot today." Jen checks her watch and grabs her bag off the table.

"Mmm, me too. I've got headshots at a marketing firm downtown." Leah pretends to gag and waves at me over her shoulder. "Have fun being gay tonight!"

"Thank you?" I call back to a suddenly empty apartment.

For the next hour, I sit quietly, pondering every time in my life I've *wanted* something and trying to decipher if anything of that level of intensity was ever felt towards a person. I definitely got butterflies in eighth grade when James Tonaka asked me to dance with him. But that may have been from knowing the other kids were watching us and the jealousy I could feel radiating off some of the girls who had crushes on him.

And probably because she was already on my mind, memories of Evan begin popping up like bright, fleeting flashes of a lens. Snapshots of us in my bed, falling asleep watching *Gilmore Girls* the summer between tenth and eleventh grade. The fan in the far corner of my childhood bedroom circulating the dry summer air. The count of exactly eleven seconds between oscillations, blowing the loose threads of her braid over her shoulder and the scent of her flowery shampoo in my direction.

The soft cotton of her pyjamas under my hand when I was trying to pry the remote away from her when she insisted on putting on *The Bachelor* come nine p.m.

Her laughing as she held it extended far enough away that I had to climb on top of her to reach it. The way my heart sank when she froze under me. The awkward pause when we both looked down at our laps, pressed together. The moment I rolled off her, claiming not to care what we watched anyway.

But that wasn't *desire*, right? That was just a strange, fleeting moment of...

Would I have let her kiss me? Did I want to kiss her?

I imagine it. What could have happened if I hadn't rolled off her lap right away.

Her hipbones digging into the inside of my thighs as I straddled her. Exploring each other's bodies with tongues and wandering hands until our matching cotton pyjama shorts came off. Soft hands. Evan's hands. My hands. Everywhere.

Her hair wrapped around us both as we'd meld into one. Me pressing gentle, sweet kisses down her spine and back up, unclasping her bra along the way. My knuckles caressing her collarbone, assisting the straps off her shoulders. Then I'd have moved my hand downward to—

A horn blares outside, and I'm submerged back into my body like an ice bath. I attempt to catch my breath, unaware that I'd been panting at my dining table, lost in a memory that never was.

"Oh, I've fucked up," I whisper to myself, wiping the faintest bit of sweat off my brow. "Shit, shit, shit," I chant, gripping on to the roots of my hair in two fists.

That may have been the most turned on I've ever been.

I'm either a narcissist—and can only get off using my *own* imagination by *myself*—or I'm not as straight as I thought I was this morning. Hell, an hour ago.

I might have a crush on my fake girlfriend.

Eight

Evan

I haven't been able to focus since lunch. At first, I thought it was a natural reaction to seeing Natalie. Not only seeing her but hearing her borderline talk shit about me in *our* place of work *with* the woman she left me for. Because that'd be enough to set me off on any given day. But strangely, that wasn't the vision playing on repeat while my students ran amuck this afternoon.

Nor is it the memory I'm reliving now either, snuggled up with Bagel on the couch.

It's Clara's voice I'm repeating on a loop. The way she sounded after just waking up. Most of the time, she speaks like there isn't enough time to get everything out. One thought poured out after another, sometimes so on top of each other it's hard to keep up. But today was different. Husky and breathy and slow. Raspy and, I know I shouldn't think this but... sexy.

I keep hearing her say *baby* over and over. The little hiccup laughs between each flirty exchange when she thought she was on speaker. That's the sobering thought I keep having to remind myself of. She stopped the act the *moment* I let her know that no one else could hear. Because *it was* just an act.

We haven't even been physically in the same room since we made our arrangement, and I'm already realising it may have been a very stupid idea. And, yes, I'm aware it was *my* idea. I'd argue that my heart is not usually such a foolish organ. Differentiating between real and fake and responding in kind didn't sound difficult. But when she spoke to me like *that*, in *that* voice—I momentarily forgot it wasn't real. And I felt... things. Turned-on things. Little twinges of a crush long buried rising back to the surface.

Which, while ridiculous, is perhaps not a feeling to ignore. So I've made a new plan. I will make my girlfriend-debut tonight. I'll show up for her the way she showed up for me this morning, get her coworkers talking, and then call off our agreement. Before things get messier.

She'll understand. Clara always understands.

With that being said, I should make a definite effort for tonight. The performance Clara gave over the phone would have fooled anyone, and I owe her big-time for that. Plus, she somehow *did* distract me from the most anxiety-inducing situation imaginable.

I slip Bagel off my lap, fetch my hair curler and makeup bag from under my bathroom sink, and put on another past episode of *The Bachelorette* on my laptop. Angling my bedroom mirror just right, I can sit on the edge of the bed and do my makeup without having to wear my glasses intermittently.

An hour later, there have been two one-on-one dates, a group date, and a mass dumping, and I'm looking like the best possible version of myself. Hair curled in a way that looks effortless yet chic, bangs shaped so they look intentional and could *almost* pass as being cut by a professional. I kept my makeup to a minimum: just a cat eye, red lip, and light coverage that gives me a dewy, soft complexion.

I look so good that someone might actually think I was able to pull a woman like Clara. That thought alone makes pride swell up in my chest.

After making an order for takeout sushi, I pull out every dress I own and toss them onto the bed. Rifling through my underwear drawer, I find another pair of black tights to replace my ripped ones. I put on a dark grey sweater dress, cinch it with a leather belt at the waist, throw on some simple stud earrings and, lastly, slip on black leather boots to match the belt.

I check myself out in the mirror one last time, reapply my ruby red lipstick, then shrug on my velvet-lined winter coat for the cold walk towards takeout and the gallery.

Nine

Clara

My hands are out in front of me, thumbs and index fingers extended into L-shapes, framing the piece Laurence and I just hung on the wall for the tenth time. He whines softly, and I shush him while waving a hand over my shoulder.

"Clarice! No!" He knows that isn't my name, but he claims his "thing" is calling everyone here by a slightly different variation of their real name. Heather is Heathen, for example, which, after knowing her for a few weeks, is kinda perfect. Loretta stays Loretta, however.

"Hush! It needs to be perfect," I retort.

"I did not take a job at a gallery to do physical labour." Laurence folds his arms, barely contained by his black denim jacket, across his chest and steadies me with a *try me* stare. "Go make yourself busy." He shoos me away just as I hear a soft tapping knock on the front door.

"Oh, I will." I wiggle my eyebrows at him and turn on my heel towards Evan and the bag of delicious food waiting for me outside. Once my back is turned to him, I take a deep breath, centering myself as best as I can. *This stunning creature waiting for you is your girlfriend! You kiss her all the time and like to rub your bits together.*

What? No!

I should probably watch some girl-on-girl porn or something to at least understand the logistics of what I'm pretending to enjoy. Additionally, that *certain* kind of research may help me figure out my sexuality. Which I need to do *fast*—to ensure Evan did *not* enter into this agreement with me under false pretences.

Awesome. I'm either lying to Loretta or Evan. Arguably the two most important women in my life at the moment.

I unlock the door and step aside, letting Ev in. "Oh, hey," I elongate the word, holding the *y* for far too long. "Hey, lovely." I go onto my toes to kiss her cheek. Peach soft. "Thank you for getting dinner." I take the to-go bag from her, which frees up her hand for me to hold. My fingers intertwine with hers, and I'm suddenly aware of every millimetre of skin on the palm of my hand. It's as if I can feel the pulse on her wrist echoing against mine—sounding off like an alarm blaring *we are touching*!

When our hands are entirely wrapped together, she gives me one tight squeeze—bringing me back into the room.

I clear my throat. "This is Laurence Nightingale. Laurence, this is my girlfriend, Evan."

"Bitch, that is *not* my last name." He extends his arm to Evan, who, while yet to say anything, meets his hand in a firm shake. "Is she also lying about your name too?"

Evan shakes her head, relaxing her shoulders simultaneously. "No, Evan is short for Evangeline, but I prefer—"

"Evangeline. Pleasure to meet you." Laurence looks between me and the sushi in my hand twice, a polite smile with an upturned chin.

"You too." Evan points to the chairs in the far corner of the room, the only ones in the building. They're entirely impractical in their lowness and curvature, but it beats the floor. "Want to join us? I picked up more than enough."

He demurely shakes his head. "No, thank you. I have dinner plans." The heels of Laurence's boots are loud as he walks away, heading up the stairs to the office and loft area above. "You're done for the night, Clara. Eat and get out!" he shouts over his shoulder once he reaches the top step.

Evan flashes her eyes at me, and I giggle in turn. "Hi," she whispers, looking down at our hands—still wrapped around each other.

"Hi." I release my bottom lip from between my teeth, just realizing it's been stuck there. "Thank you for dinner."

"If you *are* done for the night, we could go to mine. I'm not far, and I have a couch and actual chairs." Evan's brows furrow as she eyes the sitting area.

"Uh, sure. Okay."

"Unless you want to stick around to…" She winks as if she's never once done it before, and I can't help but laugh at her expense. I've always found her dorkiness absolutely adorable, but now I think maybe I find it sexy too? It could be the outfit. *How did I not notice before? Is it too late to compliment her now? She's dressed like a sexy librarian meets American Girl doll.*

"No, I thought more people would be around tonight. It's fine. Laurence is a big gossip—word will get around. Um..." I remove my hand from hers and point to the door. "I'll just get my things."

"Clara?" She tugs on the back of my blazer as I turn away.

"Hmm?" I answer, spinning back around.

Suddenly, she's closer. Her arm wrapped around the small of my back, a hip pressed to mine. Her breath against my jaw, ear pressed to my cheek, lemongrass scented shampoo flooding my senses.

"Laurence is watching us from up there," Evan whispers. "Wrap your hand around me."

"*Oh.*" I can feel the pricking of my skin across my neck, the tingling sensation that follows, my hair now standing on end as I place one hand on the hollow of her waist.

The sound of my heartbeat is so loud I can feel it pulsing against my eardrum, drowning out all other noise.

Ever so slowly, Evan spreads her fingers on the small of my back wider and moves her hand upwards. I feel muscles twitch and go rigid around my entire body as she presses on along a path towards my neck, which is unconsciously stretching to meet her.

My throat tightens just as she reaches my shoulder, then even more when her thumb rubs across the skin under my hairline. I take two inhales in a row, struggling to focus. I force out a breathy exhale that makes Evan turn to see if I'm okay. I nod silently, lips parting.

"Clara, I..." She says my name like she never has. Angry, almost. Forced out and agitated. I look up at her through heavy lashes, and her eyes are locked on my lips. A heavy expression on her face, similar to regret.

"Do you want to kiss me?" I ask.

I don't know what comes over me, but the second I watch Evan's frustration wash away into surprise, I lean in and kiss her before she's even answered. As if it was the only thing either of us could imagine doing next.

She breathes out, long and warm, against my top lip and inhales even sharper when I change the angle of our mouths slightly, pressing more fervently against her.

My top lip fits so perfectly between hers, it's damn near relaxing. Like finding the perfect position in bed to fall asleep in and feeling yourself slowly drift away.

Because I imagine it from Laurence's vantage point, it's almost as if I'm having an out-of-body experience, seeing it from a bird's-eye view.

Her merlot lips, plush and swollen, wrapped around my own. Her hand, now brushing the hair on the back of my head, so comforting that I unconsciously decide to do the same with hers where it falls down the side of her face. Evan's hair tickles my palm and entangles around my fingers like vines around a tree stump, and I tug a little. Because I've lost the ability to care, apparently, and everything in me is asking for *more.*

Just as I think it's time to pull away, some rationality coming back into the foggy atmosphere around us, Evan releases the smallest noise from the back of her throat. A mewling hum that acts as a magnet for my other hand. I drop the bag of food onto the floor, desperate to touch the other side of her face too and hold her closer.

But Evan pulls away, jumping back to look at the takeout at our feet and wincing. She steps back even farther, wiping her smeared lipstick with her thumb, her wild eyes scanning me for reassurance.

I can't close my mouth, horrified by whatever force just took over me and had me sucking my best friend's lip between my own. I want to smile at her, set her at ease. Mostly, I want to find some humour to deflect with, but I can't seem to find a single funny thing about what just occurred between us.

This was all supposed to be pretend.

But has any first kiss ever felt like *that*? Any kiss?

Not for me.

Ten

Evan

What in the flying fuck was that?

That was our *first* kiss? Our practice round? Our throwaway? Our... fuck! I can't think of any more words. What is happening? Clara must have felt that too, right?

I'm supposed to be the calm one. I've kissed plenty of women. This wasn't going to be a big deal for me. But shit, I didn't think I would kiss her tonight, and I was totally unprepared for when she... she kissed *me,* I think.

I'm picking up our food off the floor and scanning the room for cameras so I can potentially ask for playback footage when I hear Clara call from the entrance.

"Ready?" she asks, throwing her long trench coat on and fastening a page-boy hat to her head. As I approach, she's looking at her feet. Then my feet, the plant next to me, the art over my shoulder. Everywhere but my face.

"Um, yeah. Let's go."

The walk back to my place has, so far, been filled with typical city noises but no conversation. Walking under streetlamps, I take advantage of the intermittent low light and sneak glances at her. Her posture is so straight that she could be smuggling a metre stick down the seam of her coat. Whatever thoughts are running through her head right now have her presenting this more rigid, uptight version of herself.

Which leads me to believe that our kiss freaked her out.

I'd perhaps feel more guilty about that if I'd kissed her and not the other way around.

Because she definitely kissed me, right? I really should have asked Laurence for the security tapes before we left.

Fluffy snow begins falling a few minutes away from my place. It's not the kind that sticks and stays for long, but the snow globe type that is beautiful to watch. I want to ask Clara if she remembers how excited she used to get for the first snow. Whether she realised that I'd always build my snowmen in the front yard so that if she drove past with her parents, she'd see it. How much effort I put into them, hoping to impress her.

When we arrived at my building, it momentarily felt like the worst was over—but I was wrong. The lobby door shut, and we were left in total silence. Making it near painful. But what would I even say? I try the first thing I can think of.

"I got a little bit of everything," I say softly as the elevator doors close.

"Huh?" The corner of her lip juts out.

"Sushi. I got, um, a variety."

"Oh, great."

"Do you have... a favourite kind?" I ask.

"Of sushi?"

"Yeah. I like salmon and avocado the best."

"I like mostly everything. Just not, uh... yam."

"Right."

Twenty-one seconds later—yes, I counted—the doors open to my floor.

Clara follows closely behind me towards my apartment, and we're greeted by Bagel—who's probably only interested in us for the raw fish we've brought home.

"Don't let his friendliness fool you." I scratch the back of my neck after removing my coat and hanging it up. "He's after our food."

Clara hangs her coat up next to mine, then slides off her ankle boots. She's wearing white socks with small strawberries on them.

"Those are cute." I point to her feet, stuck looking at the ground between us. This awkwardness is next-level torture.

She steps closer until her socks are nearly touching the tip of my tights. I don't look up. Can't yet.

"I think we should kiss some more." Clara says this so confidently, so concisely, I feel like I missed the rationale.

I slowly move my eyes to her face, letting myself take in her body along the way. "Okay... for practice or...?"

"Science." Her nose crinkles in the mischievous way it did when we were kids getting into trouble. This, certainly, is trouble.

"You want to kiss me for science, Teens?" I have to laugh. Just a little.

Her hand grips mine tightly as she keeps her eyes locked on me. "I'm not sure what's going on with me," she whispers. "But I think I like it."

"Kissing girls?"

"Kissing *you*," she quickly retorts. "I was doing some thinking today..." She plays with my fingers in hers, tracing up and around my palm with her thumb. "This doesn't feel nearly as strange as it should, right? I've never really wanted this before," her laugh is half a sigh, "but this... this feels so..."

"Easy?" I offer.

"I was going to go with *exhilarating*, but sure."

I bite down on my smile as her eyes fixate on my mouth. "That's awfully gay of you, Clara."

"Ya think?" Her teasing smile matches my own.

"I think I like this too," I say decidedly.

"What?" She tilts her head, her brows furrowing slightly.

"Kissing you." I swallow. "I think I like it a lot."

She rocks backs on her heels, smiling at the ground between us. "Okay, so do something about—"

I cut Clara off by reaching for her jaw, tilting her face upwards, and slotting my mouth against hers. More feverishly this time because I'm a little too eager. I lean back, silently apologising for the aggression, but when she whines and pulls me back with a grip on my neck, I give into the wanting.

"Let's sit," I say between kisses, my mouth incapable of leaving hers for very long.

She nods, following my step as I walk backwards and clumsily into my couch. Clara shakes her blazer off until it lands on the floor behind us. I run my hands from her wrists to her shoulders, loving that I have more of her skin available to me.

When I sit, she sort of falls on top of me, as if she also can't bear the idea of our lips not touching. Eventually, we find a more comfortable position with her legs on either side of mine, straddling me.

"I was thinking about this today," she whispers against my neck, kissing my jaw. "Do you remember when I did this before? We were—"

"The remote." Of course I remember. How could I possibly forget my several-year-crush sitting on my lap, even for half a second?

Clara shifts backwards, her eyes searching mine.

"I remember," I say, grabbing hold of the back of her knees, the soft linen fabric of her trousers barely a layer between my hands and her thighs. She smiles as I pull her closer. "A little surprised you do." I kiss her shoulder, then wrap my lips around her collarbone and revel in the rewarding sound of her gasping moans.

Clara likes having her chest kissed.

Clara is on my lap.

Clara remembers the time she was on my lap, when I thought my little queer teenage heart was going to fracture and burst.

Clara and I have a *lot* to talk about.

"Is this happening too fast? Should we...?" I ask, sort of.

"Slow down?" Clara nods once, twice, then tilts her head as if she's unsure. She nods once more but then begins shaking it, laughing quietly. "I mean, I think I should say yes and stop, but honestly, this is all very new for me, and I feel like I have a lot to catch up on here so..."

A laugh escapes me, but it's quickly put to rest when Clara begins unbuttoning her blouse. "Unless you want to?" she asks me, hands stilling on her fourth button, her purple lace bra peeking through.

Partially because words seem to fail me at the moment, but also because I'm desperate too, I lean forward and place a chaste kiss above her breast. Looking up as far as I can, straining my neck, I watch her lips part and suck in a breath as my bottom lip traces the trim of her bra.

Both of her hands move to the back of my head, showing me that she really wants me to keep kissing her there. I make quick work of undoing the rest of her buttons and sliding off her shirt. Every new revelation of her skin, areas previously unseen and certainly untouched, lull me further into a sensation of dreaming.

Perhaps because I've dreamed about this so many more times than I'd ever admit out loud.

This is Clara. Teens. Daryl and Maggie's daughter. My friend. Incredible photographer. The most stunning woman alive. With me. Touching me. Moaning after each of my kisses.

The thought makes me a little dizzy, and I pull back.

"You okay?"

"I think I'm feeling a bit lightheaded." I swallow my pride, looking up at her.

She nods. Disappointment flashing across her features.

And there it is... the same look Natalie gave me time and time again. Another reason our relationship fell apart. *Fuck.*

Sometimes sex can become a bit too much for me. I've been known to shut down. The feeling of too much touching, kissing, overheating. Things I ought to enjoy paralyse me.

Just as I'm about to string together a long line of apologies and explanations, Clara speaks.

"Let's go lie down." She hops off my lap and pulls me up with her hand around mine. Topless Clara is now leading me to my bedroom, and I follow her, stunned. Shit, I never moved the dresses off my bed.

"Couldn't narrow it down?" She smiles over her shoulder. I shrug, eyes entirely focused on the shifting muscle in her shoulder as she surveys the room.

"You're so beautiful, Clara." The words fall out of me.

She turns to me, takes a step closer, and lays one flat palm on my cheek. "I don't think I've truly ever felt that way until tonight... thank you."

"I think I'm just catching up, ya know? This is a big change, and while it's amazing, it's also—"

Clara interrupts my spiral with a chaste kiss. She's not turned off. She's not running away. Thank God. "Let's just lie down. Do you still like to be tucked in when you feel... overwhelmed?"

I stare at her in disbelief as she takes all the dresses off my bed, hangs them up, then begins rearranging pillows. "Climb in," she says.

I move slowly, studying her calm expression as I do. Is she not annoyed? She said she wanted to kiss more, and we did, but I doubt she was done. Hell, I didn't want to be.

While I shift under the covers, Clara puts a few pillows around me like a barricade. "I'm just gonna go put the food in your fridge before Bagel swoops in." I nod, sort of amazed by the ease with which she's taking care of me. And the fact that I don't feel all that embarrassed. A moment later, she's back and getting into bed.

"Want to watch *The Bachelor* or something?" She cuddles up next to me, her blond hair cascading over my shoulder. "Is this okay?"

This is *better* than okay. This is better than anything. "Yes... and yes."

We watch an entire episode, making small talk about the contestants. When the credits roll and the next episode comes up, I hit Select, then Pause on the remote. "I'm sorry, and I'm sorry it took me an hour to say that."

"You have no reason to be sorry." She sits up, pinning me flat against the mattress with her stern but caring expression. "Really."

"I love kissing you. I really want to keep doing that at some point," I state plainly. I want her to know. Need her to.

She smiles, bright and wide and contagious. "Good." She lies back down, reaches across my lap, and hits Play. "Does that mean I can sleep over?"

I kiss her forehead and breathe her in, smiling down at her chest splayed across me. "Yes, please."

Eleven

Clara

At some point, long after we'd both fallen asleep, Evan let me know she was ready to kiss again. It started with a delicate finger across my collarbone and a quiet "you awake?" And while I'd technically not been, that didn't matter anymore. Sleep could wait.

We kissed long and slow, both lying down and tucked in our separate, cosy blanket cocoons. Eventually, we merged blankets, my fingertips finding the fabric of her dress to grip on to, hers digging into the flesh at my waist.

Every little evolution of our kiss started with a whispered, sincere question. "Are you sure?" I'd help her out of her tights. "Do you like that?" I'm sliding my tongue against hers. "Is this okay?" She's reaching for my ass. "Do you want to…?" A question I never finished but we both understood. I removed my trousers while she removed her dress. Side by side, we stripped down to our underwear.

Now, we're pressed all over. Grasping hands and sliding knees, hooking around each other and finding friction. While I know I'm nearly thirty and this may sound absurd, it's all so new.

Feelings I'd suspected existed but never felt are suddenly real. Tangible and heavy. A giddy, excited, and lustful wanting. And I can feel myself getting wetter, rubbing the seam of my panties over her thigh as she slides her knee up and under me.

She's responsive too. Not just with the little whimpers of approval she makes but with how she somehow seems to know what I want. The slow kisses back and forth across my collarbones, the sucking on the base of my neck. Her hand holding mine, clasped and pressed above my head into the mattress.

She's been on top for a while now, and I suspect it should be my turn to roll us and take control, but my bones have all melted. That's her fault. I blame her.

"Clara..." She whispers my name into my neck, her hand grabbing hold of my waist. "Can I go down on you?"

"If—if you'd like," I stutter, going mindless yet again under her intoxicating pull. The top of my breast between her teeth mixed with the tips of her hair tickling me all over my chest.

She raises to look at me, a question and smirk in her expression. "It's definitely more about whether you'd like me to." She kisses me just once, and I groan as she moves away. "Would you like me to?" she asks, chest heaving.

I squint, unsure of whether each confession of inexperience makes me seem less desirable to her. "No one's ever done that before," I whisper.

"Nobody?" She leans in and kisses me from my ear to jaw to mouth as I shake my head. "Because you said no?" she asks.

"Because they never asked."

"I'm asking," she says, voice more breath than words, and sits up to gauge my reaction.

"Okay." I giggle, which should feel embarrassing—but I think Evan's too busy relishing in my answer to care. Her eyes suddenly hooded and blazing. "What do I do?" I ask.

"Nothing. Um, well, tell me what feels good. If something doesn't, correct me."

I swallow. "Okay."

"Can I take this off first?" She palms my bra, pinching my nipple through the thin fabric.

"Only if I can take yours off too." I reach up and pull the straps into two hands, toying with them.

I lift, allowing her to help me slide mine off over my head as I unclasp hers. Her bra falls forward, and she slips her arms out, tossing it off the bed. I grab a hold of her neck and bring her back down to me, pressing her body against mine. The feeling of skin on skin, breast touching breast, is so exhilarating that my body begins writhing against her—seeking out friction between my legs.

I don't know what I'm doing. I also don't know how I'd identify myself at this point. But I *do* know that there isn't a label, self-realisation, or epiphany that matters as much as how good this feels. If I had to pinpoint it—if I was asked at this exact moment—I'd say my sexuality is the corner of Evan's lips. It's the gasps she makes that act as a windstorm in my chest. It's the space between her fingers where I fit better than anywhere else. It's all instinct here. Intuition. And I've been waiting my whole life for this rush. So I'm not questioning it anymore.

Evan begins lowering herself down my body. First giving attention to my tits, sucking my nipples into her mouth and rolling them over with her tongue. I clasp so tightly on to her hair that I worry I'm hurting her. But that's when she bites, making me squeal. So I tug harder.

My hips begin raising off the bed, like they have a mind of their own and are begging to be let in on the action. The action being her mouth. Her fucking mouth! How does she kiss like this? How does she—

"Whoa." I grab her shoulder as she swipes her tongue just below my navel and bites down on the band of my panties.

"Still yes?" she asks, fabric between her teeth.

"Oh my god, yes." I laugh, breathless and needy.

She hooks her tongue under the seam of my underwear and kisses sweetly from hip to hip—mimicking the sensation against my collarbones that drove me crazy. If that was enough for me to lose all sense of control before, then I think I've elevated to a new level of wanting.

I use two thumbs to slide my underwear down, lifting off the bed as Evan positions herself between my knees, kissing each one tenderly.

I allow myself a moment of utter gratitude, realising how easy this feels. Sex before felt like having to perform in front of an audience and panel of judges. Sex with Evan feels like I've known all the steps all along, like a memory sketched into my bone marrow, for only us. Our sacred ritual. Our holy land.

I lie back down, letting my head find a comfortable position on her fluffy fur pillow as Evan pulls my underwear past my ankles. Taking the arch of my foot in her hand, she follows the line of my calf muscle up, nibbling and licking my flesh along the way.

I almost tell her that I can't wait anymore, but then she lines herself up with my centre and looks up at me one last time for permission through dark lashes.

I nod maniacally. Evan grins like the devil herself, blows out a long breath, then lowers her mouth to me.

"Oh god" slips off my tongue instantly. She hums against me, a happy, approving sound. I hiss on an inhale as she pulls my clit into her mouth. Horror washes over me, my wide-opened eyes staring up at the ceiling that whirls in and out of focus. It's been less than ten seconds, and I'm about to explode. Heat pools in my belly and pressure in my spine like a rapidly fraying knot tied to an anvil.

"Wait..." I breathe out, too quiet for her to hear. Mostly because my thighs are acting as earmuffs.

"Whoa." I inhale sharply, twisting against her. She pins my hips down, curling her arm around my thighs and pressing me into the mattress with a hold on my hip. That's when she lifts her shoulder off the bed and pushes her finger inside me, curling it in a *come here* motion that sets the world on fire.

"Fuck!" I shout out. *Yes, yes, yes, yes, yes.* "Evan! Yes!" I cry out, shaking and gasping while my soul tries to leave my body behind. She's relentless, tapping a spot I didn't know existed and will definitely make her find again, watching me fall apart with careful eyes and pouty lips from between my legs.

When I finally stop shaking, Evan uses her mouth again timidly. Licking and soothing me with sweet kisses until my body fully relaxes around her.

Looking down, I find Evan resting her chin on the top of my bikini line. She's all swollen lips and glassy eyes that have me questioning how, even for a split second, let alone eighteen years, I didn't want to eat her alive. I pat her cheek and thank her profusely with giggling smiles and gentle praises.

That was amazing. You're amazing. Nothing has ever felt that good. How did you do that so quickly? Very efficient. You should do that as your job. Not that you aren't good at teaching just—

Kissing my palm, Evan smiles to herself when I stop blubbering. She climbs up the bed and settles next to me, brushing her hand in lazy circles over my abdomen for what feels like forever.

"Evan?" I whisper into the darkened room.

"Hmm?"

"That *really was* incredible."

She kisses the side of my chin and curls around me with a knee across my lap. "Good."

I smile to myself. "I think I might be gay."

"Based on recent events," she teases, "I'd have to agree."

"Does that bother you? That I'm so new to this? That I'm only figuring this out? I don't really know it all yet, but I know that I love this. I promise I'm not using you to—"

"Clara," she interrupts firmly, "orgasms are supposed to be relaxing. So either go back to sleep or let me give you another one."

"I do *not* think my body could handle that." I kiss her nose and tease her lips with a soft brush of mine.

"Then shush, please. M'sleeping," she mumbles, curling her face against my neck. I'm lulled back to sleep by the sweet sounds of her contended breaths and heavy limbs across me—tethering me to the earth.

Twelve

Evan

November 30th

You'd have thought that I'd hit her grandmother with my car and set the bed on fire with the way Clara acted when my alarm went off this morning. I *should* be offended by the ease with which she threatened my life and the well-being of my phone, but it was honestly adorable. She's too small to be actually scary. Plus I'm so far gone for her it's not even funny.

And it's *really* not funny. It's rather terrifying. Or, at least, it should be.

Clara has been the only remaining link between my old life and new for a decade, and this could absolutely end in disaster.

However—and I'm not sure what's come over me and will deny it if asked—I don't foresee this ending badly. I actually have a *really* good feeling that this could have been the first day of waking up next to the love of my life.

Even if she wants to end me prematurely for getting out of bed and waking her before ten.

She'll have to get used to it. Or, alternatively, I'll have to get used to her threats.

I text her my goodbye, sneak back into the bedroom to leave a glass of water on the bedside table, and make my way out the door.

As soon as I arrive at school, I try to switch into work mode. I've always been good at that, switching on and off when necessary. However, when my students file in, it becomes blatantly clear I'm going to struggle to focus today. They're also watching me a little too intently for my own comfort. Except I can't stop smiling.

"You're scaring me," Talia says, walking past my desk to the water fountain and side-eyeing me the whole way. "You're"—she studies me with a peaked brow—"happy."

"Did *The Bachelorette* premiere?" Another student, Carla, asks from the front row.

"No, that was last month," Michael pipes up from the back of the class. "This face is new. A different sort of happy."

I feel my cheeks redden, suddenly aware of twenty sets of eyes fixed on me. "I'm just really excited about our field trip next week."

A resounding declaration of huffed laughs, *yeah rights,* and sarcastic *pleases* answer me.

"Let me see your phone background!" Adam thumps his way over to my desk, and I decide to waive my no phone rule, as this may help my case.

"Bagel the cat." I shimmy the phone. "Really, team, if I had news, I'd tell you."

Talia turns back with her filled water bottle in hand. She takes intentionally sassy, loud sips as she passes by towards her seat.

"I think you have a girlfriend," she conspires from her desk.

"I think you still owe me two work assignments and a group project," I fire back.

The day passes slowly and arduously. The nearer we get to winter break, the more unsettled the kids get. I partially blame the Halloween candy stashes for the November attitude crash, but I also can't fault them for not wanting to be here. The students want to be home, playing video games or watching television or doing god knows what on TikTok. The cold weather calls for it. Like something in our collective genetic makeup dictates we ought to hibernate.

And after last night, I can't say I wouldn't rather be home right now, hibernating under blankets with Clara. Or using her legs as a scarf.

It's the last period of my school day when Clara sends me a photo of her at work. She's got one hand on the phone in her hip's holster, and she's wearing an overly concentrated expression. The banner across the photo reads "ready at any moment."

She's my favourite person in the world.

I pick up my whiteboard eraser, check that the kids are busy with their work, and hold it like a weapon for a quick photo. "Bring it on," I write back.

Her response comes quickly. "You're my favourite."

Glad we're on the same page, then.

EVAN: How's opening prep?

CLARA: Loretta is nowhere to be found. There are rumours she's joined a monastery in Tibet.

EVAN: Ah, naturally.

CLARA: But it's going well. I may have gotten a little hyper-fixated and finished all my tasks for the day (rest of the week). I'll be off early.

"Oh." I respond, trying to think of a better way to say *come back to mine, then, please.*

CLARA: Want to finally share that sushi?

EVAN: Nothing like day-old refrigerated sushi.

EVAN: Yes, please.

CLARA: Good. I took your spare key before I left today.

"You'll be home before me?" I reply before thinking about what the word *home* implicates.

CLARA: After I stop by my place and grab a bag. How many nights should I pack for?

EVAN: I mean, you may as well be close to work before the gallery opens. In case of emergency.

CLARA: Three nights. Got it.

EVAN: The gallery opens in two nights?

CLARA: You're right. It'd be silly to leave before the end of the weekend. Better pack for five.

I smile so brightly at my phone it feels like my jaw might break. "Five is perfect," I reply. Then, because I cannot resist, I add, "Though with the staff party being only a few days after..."

CLARA: How could I forget? I couldn't possibly leave before the work party.

EVAN: Just pack everything.

CLARA: Are we renting a U-Haul? I feel like as the newer queer in this relationship, I'm not allowed to make a joke first.

I laugh out loud, which makes a few students look up from their work. *Shit.*

EVAN: I'll see you when I get home, weirdo.

CLARA: Will Bagel have to start calling me mother right away, or do we start with Ms. Spencer? Less formal? Ms. Clara?

EVAN: Ms. Spencer, I'm going to get fired if I don't pay attention to my students now.

CLARA: Call me that in bed later ;)

I shut off my phone and throw it in my drawer for good measure. I'm so stupidly gone for her it's embarrassing. But I will *absolutely* not be calling her that.

Thirteen

Evan

When I arrive home, Bagel is not screaming, and the smell of something delicious greets me—which means Clara got here first. "Clara?" I call out, dropping my purse and backpack near the front door. I kick off my boots and follow my nose towards the sweet scent. "Hey," I call out again, turning the corner to my typical Toronto apartment kitchen. Meaning I had believed it far too tiny to bake in before now.

"Hi!" Clara exclaims, greeting me with a kiss on my cheek. She's wearing an apron she must have brought from home, and every inch of her is dusted with flour. "Welcome home," she says before winking and turning back to her work.

As if it's the most natural thing in the world for her to be here. Perhaps because it is.

"Hey," I say, a little stunned. "Baking?"

She nods excitedly while curling her index finger around the rim of a bowl, bringing the batter to her mouth, and licking it off. "Mm-hmm! I had this idea while walking here. Well, actually, several." She turns to me, her smile crooked and kid-like. "Care for a glimpse into my head?"

How do I say yes in a way that's not as desperate as I feel? "Sure."

Her face falls. I overcorrected. *Just be honest. It's Clara.*

"I want to know every thought you have, actually. I sort of hate that I can't dial in there whenever I want."

Instantly, she's back to beaming. "Okay, so. I got on the subway from the gallery, and there was a poster with a mouse on it. So naturally, I started thinking about cheese. And because I was already slightly dreading day-old sushi, I thought I'd stop at the grocery store near my house and grab stuff for a cheese plate. I had this whole image of me feeding you grapes. It was very sexy." She takes a breath for the first time since beginning her story. "Then I thought about grape juice, which made me think of grape jelly, which made me think of—"

I interrupt, my mouth agape. "Grape jelly pinwheels?"

She points at me, smiling. "Yes!"

My mom made them for *every* church potluck. It was her claim to fame. I've really fucking missed them.

"I went online and found a recipe for them, but something in my gut just said, no, that's not right." She opens my oven, ducks to look inside by bending in half, then stands up briskly to slam the oven door shut again. "So I called my mom. I guess she'd written your mom's recipe down once, so she went through her cupboards and found it and texted me a photo. I went to the store, and now I'm making them." Her smile falters. "Oh, but I didn't get anything to eat for dinner. I just realised that."

It's silly. It's honestly embarrassing, but I start to cry.

"Oh, Ev..." Clara unties the apron and tosses it onto the counter. Her arms wrap around me, and I lean into her.

"I-I just didn't think I'd get to have them again," I stutter, attempting to contain myself. "I'm happy," I sniffle, "and a little sad, I guess."

"Don't cry..." She rubs my back. "They might turn out terrible," she coos.

I laugh, wiping the last tear away. "Thank you for this, Teens."

"Hey." She reaches for me, moving my hair away from my face and looking up at me with so much tenderness I feel my heart *thud*. "Want to help me make them?"

I nod. Clara boops my nose before turning on her heel and reaching back for her apron. "Oh no! I forgot!"

I look on the counter for a clue at what she's forgotten, but then she's got her mouth pressed to mine, smiling into our kiss. "Hi, beautiful. Missed you."

Can you be here every day? Is what I want to say. "I love you being here" is what I say instead as she gets back to work measuring sugar.

The cookies turned out even better than I remembered. I told Clara this, but I don't think she believes me. She's got so many hidden talents. She claims it's from a lifetime of picking up hobbies, focusing on them until she's had her fill, then dropping them for the next best thing. Baking is just one of those things for her.

I can't wait to see each and every one of them. And watch her discover more hobbies too.

"Do you knit?" I ask. I quickly realise, based on Clara's obvious confusion, that we've sat for nearly an hour in perfect silence on my bed. We haven't been talking out loud about Clara's magnificent brain. I've just been thinking about her still.

"Nope," she says, shrugging. "Why? Did you want a blanket? A sweater?"

I chuckle, brushing my hand over her hip. "Maybe... Could be a cosy new hobby."

"Oh, I see! You're trying to use my neurodiversity to your advantage." She teases, forcing her laugh to subside as she speaks.

"Something like that." I smile, tilting her to look back up at me from where she's splayed across my chest. God, she's beautiful. "Can I kiss you?"

Her lips twitch into a smirk. "No matter how much we make out, I will not learn to knit. So don't try it."

"No, I've just been waiting for you to initiate, and I can't anymore."

Clara bites her lip while shuffling up the bed to lie next to me. "I've been waiting for you to start us off."

"We're so polite," I whisper against her lips.

"Very conscientious." She brushes her tongue over my mouth as I find her hair with my hands, tugging her closer.

We kiss forever. Not literally, obviously—we'd die—but for a very long time. And it doesn't feel overwhelming. Even when my jaw starts to hurt, it's easy to ignore.

"Ev?" Clara whispers.

"Yes?"

"Can I..." Her forehead presses into mine, and she giggles softly. "Can I... please... touch you?"

I swallow a lump in my throat. "Yeah."

"You'll have to be patient with me... I'm new." She kisses my neck, and if *that's* any indication of how this is going to work between us, I think she'll do just fine.

"That's okay."

It's a bit awkward but mostly endearing as Clara helps me out of my tights and underwear. She kisses my ankle, and I buck in response.

"Sorry. Just... not *too* gentle. Gentle touches feel a bit like an itch I can't scratch."

She nods, tightening her grip around my opposite knee. She looks across my body, then climbs back next to me, falling with a bounce. "Can we kiss until my confidence comes back?"

I nod, meeting her mouth with mine. *This* we're both *really* good at.

Minutes later, she's bunching the fabric of my dress at my hip, gathering it into her palm between panted, shared breaths. I feel my hips twisting towards her, seeking out her hand. Once she's got my dress hiked up, she places her spread palm on the top of my thigh, then squeezes.

"God, I love these."

"My legs?" I almost laugh at the sound of wonder in her voice. It's like Clara doesn't know how stunning *she* is.

"This part." She pinches the bulge around my hip. "So sexy," she breathes into my mouth.

A whine escapes from the back of my throat. "Clara…" I whisper, twisting to make her hand move where I need it. "Please."

"Okay." She nods against the side of my cheek. Her thumbnail scrapes across my flesh in the most sensational way until she reaches pubic hair and briefly pauses. "I like this too." She smiles, petting the coarse hair.

"You're killing me." I laugh without joy, tugging her to my mouth, knowing that will make her hand drop just a little. It does. And it's like Clara suddenly remembers that she *too* has a vagina, because she does *exactly* the right thing.

"This?" she asks, spreading wetness up to my most sensitive spot with one finger.

"Mmm," I hum, voice pitching up and tensing. "Yes," I breathe out as she starts making slow, delicate circles. "Harder though."

She does as told, and my back arches off the bed.

"Wow," she whispers, igniting a fire in my belly. "Wow," she says again, more reverently, before she dives to kiss my mouth and adds another finger, pinching my clit between them.

"Clara," I gasp. "Clara, that's so fucking good."

I kiss her just once before she shocks us both, based on her wide-eyed expression of near horror. She's got those same two fingers between her lips, sucking my taste into her mouth.

She blinks rapidly three times, her hand falling between us. "Wow."

"You keep saying that," I tease.

"Can I?" She licks her lips, her hooded eyes watching me intently after flicking down the bed to my parted legs.

"Yes."

She's moving down the bed so quickly it's hard *not* to giggle at her eagerness.

And this woman thought she was straight less than a week ago.

Clara starts slowly again, fingering me in the most teasing, most delicious way that has my breath coming in short and praises slipping off my tongue effortlessly. It's mindless and perfect but not enough to actually come.

Then she kisses that same spot below my hip she admitted to loving earlier. Her teeth skate towards my thigh. Then lingering kisses just above my pubic hair before her hands both move to my knees, pushing them apart as she gets comfortable between them.

"Wow," she says again, barely above a whisper, just before she's pressed up against my pussy. Her mouth, nose, and tongue all active participants.

"Clara," I moan out, grabbing hold of the sheet with a fist and instinctively sitting up to watch. "That's perfect, honey." I reach and hold her golden hair in my fist. Fuck, this is *Clara Spencer.* My never-to-be crush. My dream girl. Eating me out like she's never tasted something quite as good. I get a little prideful at that, pulling on her hair as if to say *mine*.

She's so fucking good at this. I'd be a little mad if I wasn't the beneficiary of her natural skill. Jealous that she picked up yet another thing so easily.

A deep moan crawls up my throat as she makes a sound like slurping against me. She's really enjoying this. Enjoying *me*. That thought alone has my toes curling and fists tightening as she leads me expertly over the edge into oblivion with her tongue pressing in languid circles.

She doesn't stop until I'm screaming her name over and over. Begging like I've never begged before for her to stop—or keep going—in a torturous cycle.

Fourteen

Clara

December 2nd

After three blissful days of flirting via text, watching reality TV, working, and remembering to eat between make-out sessions, it's the gallery's winter open. And while I'd love to pretend I'm some sort of method-actress, committed to this part she accidentally auditioned for, pretending to be Evan's girlfriend isn't pretending at all anymore.

It's actually the easiest role I've ever taken on.

New revelations that I've had in the past seventy-two hours include, but are not limited to: the thirteenth season of *The Bachelorette* is far better than the rest, Evan loves my tits a *lot*, and I'm actually quite good at eating out women. Ev told me I have a *natural* gift. I was pretty content with that review. Though I don't think there's any way she enjoyed it more than I enjoyed doing it for the first time. Or the second or the third... or the fourth.

It's quickly become my absolute favourite thing in the world.

After tonight, the focus will be on getting Evan through the hellish experience of her ex-fiancée's holiday party next week. Then, it *should* be relatively smooth sailing until I leave for my parents' house. But even though I can't wait to see them both and fulfil our Spencer holiday traditions, I'm already dreading leaving Evan for the holidays.

Maybe she'd come with me if it wasn't the very place she's been avoiding for ten years. I can't truly imagine what Ev feels when she thinks about our hometown. I know it can't be the same warm, glowing, safe nostalgia that I feel. I imagine it's more like disappointment. Betrayal, even. The people who made you, who are supposed to love you, abandoning you.

Even still, she must not want to be home alone for Christmas. If we went to my parents' together, we could hibernate. She'd not have to see or do anything she didn't want to. We could just be together. There's no harm in asking… right? I wouldn't want her to not have the choice or feel welcome. I'll ask her. After tonight though. One thing at a time.

"Ready?" Evan calls out from the living room as I finish touching up my makeup in front of the bathroom mirror.

"Ready," I call back, opening the door and giving her a small turn. My black dress with a tattered tutu-style bottom flounces as I do. Evan's eyes bulge, and I watch her lips quirk into a giddy smile as she takes me in.

"You look adorable."

"What? No!" I drop my shoulders. "I was going for chic." I study the dress, playing with the hem.

"Yes. Chic, obviously," Evan overcorrects. "You look formidable."

"How bad is it?" I sigh, begging her with my eyes to soften the blow.

"You look *beautiful*, Clara."

I wince, seeing myself in her hallway's full-length mirror. "No! I look like I'm about to go sit on Santa's knee."

She comes up behind me and wraps her hands around my waist. She tucks her chin over my shoulder, and we both look into the mirror. Evan's wearing a vintage-style navy dress that's fitted on top with a silky skirt past her knees. Hot teacher vibes for *sure*. And way out of my *dressed-like-a-toddler* league.

"Clara, the dress is perfect. You're perfect."

"It's childish."

"It's joyful. It's fun. Like you."

"The people coming to this thing will think I'm a joke." I tilt my head into hers, pouting at my reflection.

"Let them. We know the truth. Loretta does. Next year, when it's *your* art and not Heather's, they'll see it too. I think this is my favourite dress you've ever worn." She kisses my cheek and straightens, putting her hands inside her coat pocket. "And I cannot *wait* to peel it off you later." Her eyes drift down my back slowly.

I fix my shoulders and face myself head-on, the picture of confidence. "Yeah, okay." I slide my heeled ankle boots on, let Evan help me into my coat, and kiss her as we walk out the door towards the gallery. Thank goodness I've got an *actual* date.

When we arrive, it's just staff, their dates, and what I imagine are the fellow vampires Heather was spawned alongside that she calls friends. Loretta is upstairs, pacing in the conference room. Once we've checked our coats and grabbed a cocktail and an appetiser or two, I leave Evan with Laurence and make my way upstairs.

Knocking on the glass door, I wait for Loretta's signal before entering.

"Well, you look precious." She gestures to me with both hands before clasping them in front of her. "Like a little doll."

I cringe but attempt to turn it into a smile. "Thank you. You look wonderful." I gesture to her fitted tuxedo. "How are you doing? Do you need anything?"

"No, I'm just... waiting up here to make a grand entrance." She rolls her eyes at herself. "My wife is downstairs. She refuses to play along with my bravado. Or miss out on an open bar." She stares below with fondness in her eye.

I laugh, joining her at the farthest wall from the entrance that looks out over the party.

"That's her." She points to a woman with blazing red hair who's wearing a near identical outfit to Loretta's. "My Inessa."

I watch as she slips past Evan to wrap her arm around Laurence's shoulder. They kiss on the cheek in greeting, and he introduces her to Evan, who shakes her hand.

"That's Evan," I say, my pride similar to Loretta's.

"She's stunning." Loretta looks back towards me. "How did you two meet?"

"Childhood, actually. Our parents attended the same church."

Loretta's eyes flare. "*Oh.*"

I laugh, just once. "Yeah. Nothing happened until very recently between us. We, um, well, I was... a late bloomer?" I crinkle my nose, and Loretta smiles mercifully.

"Maybe for the best, given how you met?"

"Well, my parents would never have cared."

"But Evan's?"

"They cared a lot. Too much." I stop myself from sharing Evan's story any further.

"Such a shame." Loretta sighs, crossing her arms. Her eyes land nowhere in particular below as more people funnel into the gallery. "To have a child and not accept every facet of them."

I nod. "I should be getting back downstairs. Unless...?"

"No, I'm fine. Enjoy the party. Introduce me to Evan later, okay? Keep her away from Heather," Loretta teases with a smile.

"Will do." I take one step before Loretta mumbles to herself and laughs. I hesitate to inquire, but curiosity gets the better of me, and I turn around.

She smiles at her feet. "You know, it's silly. When you mentioned a *girlfriend* on your first day here, well," she laughs, "at the risk of sounding entirely ridiculous—the *old* lesbian that I am—I thought you simply meant a friend that was a girl."

I can't help it. The laugh that escapes me is a shocked, obnoxious thing. Half snorting, half disbelief. And it goes on for way too long before I manage to contain it.

"Is it *that* silly of me?" She tilts her head, looking at me conspicuously.

"Loretta," I choke through a laugh, "I think it's time I set the record straight…"

Fifteen

Clara

"You told her?" Evan glances over my shoulder at Loretta, who's greeting some new arrivals. "Just flat out told her the truth?"

"I did." I take a sip of mulled wine. "I mean, Loretta *loved* the story. I think she considers herself responsible. She says she wants to officiate our wedding someday." The words slip out, and I shut my mouth tight. "She was joking, obviously."

You're going to scare her off.

"Only if she wears that sweet suit." Evan takes a sip, like nothing either of us said is absurd. So I kiss her. Just briefly, at the risk of not being able to stop once we start. A *thank you* sort of kiss.

I love that there are no games between us. No carefully chosen words. No unspoken thoughts. Just honest, blunt enthusiasm for what's to come. It's freeing to not have to pretend.

"We have to mingle for another hour or so. After Loretta makes her speech, we can get going," I say as Evan checks the time on her watch.

"Sorry, it's a nervous habit."

"Don't be. I'm just grateful you're here. I know it's a lot." I take her hand in mine and pull her over to the smaller exhibition room. There's a small crowd in here, but it's a lot quieter. Nothing but hushed chatter as folks admire the photographs. A room filled with tilted heads and narrowed eyes. Some scowling, some appreciative. It's everything I love most about being in a gallery—watching other people take it all in. Deciphering what they think.

"Heather is very talented," Evan whispers, admiring the photograph entitled, *inferno overpass.*

You guessed it—it's a bridge on fire.

"I'm not entirely convinced she just *stumbled* across that fire," I whisper back.

We side-step over to the next photo and the one after that too. Sharing quick glances and appreciative nods with one another.

Heather comes around, greeting the guests. I introduce her to Evan, and Heather actually smiles. Once she's moved on, I tell Evan just how rare that is and watch her prideful smirk grow.

Overall, the evening goes smoothly. Heather will most likely receive warm accolades, and Loretta will be able to boast about another successful winter showcase. And I got to be a part of it. That's pretty fucking cool.

When we eventually leave and make our way to Evan's through the cruel onslaught of snow, I'm on cloud nine.

It's not my art this year, but it will be someday—maybe next year. I've got the world's most incredible woman accompanying me and a warm blanket on *her* bed waiting for me that I've claimed as my own. Plus a cat I've grown quite fond of, despite his yelling tendencies. Life is good. There's only one thing I want—Ev home with me for the holidays.

Evan takes the first shower as I make us some popcorn for tonight's final episode of—you'll *never* guess— *The Bachelorette*. She was willing to miss watching it live, but not without insisting we watch it the moment we got home, no matter what time.

I have a shower once she's done. After scrubbing all the makeup and Toronto grime off myself, I curl in bed next to her. We're both fitted with matching towels in our hair and accompanying fluffy robes. I'm sure we look like some sort of adorable, inclusive *Ikea* advertisement.

We fast forward through the first few commercials before I introduce the idea of kissing during them instead. Right when I think I've convinced her to keep kissing and stop watching entirely, the host croons that it's time for the men to pick out rings. I might be more upset if not for the fact that watching Evan enjoy anything this much is just as fun for me.

It's the way her face lights up. The little stims she does with the tapping of her fingers against mine or the wiggling of her toes under our blanket. She's so happy. I'd do *anything* to keep it that way.

The next commercial break comes, and Evan turns to me, smiling, readying to be inundated by kisses. Instead, I brush my thumb over her soft upper lip and gather my courage. "What are you and Bagel doing for Christmas break?" I ask.

Evan smirks under my thumb, then attempts to make her face stern. "Bagel doesn't celebrate Christmas."

"My apologies," I correct, smiling fiercely. "What are you and Bagel doing for the *holidays*?"

"This." Evan shrugs. "But, without you, I guess." She pouts, reaching for my hand on top of the covers.

"Would you maybe want to come back home with me? Stay with my parents?" I ask, as gentle as I can. And I know it's a serious proposition because Evan hits Pause on the remote.

She looks down between us, a heavy expression overtaking her, pulling down on her features. "Teens... I don't know," she answers softly.

"I know it might feel scary, but you *deserve* to go back home. No one should be shut out of the community they grew up in. And I want you there."

"I wouldn't want to see them," she says adamantly, her face immediately fearful.

I nod vigorously, protectiveness propelling me. "Then we absolutely won't."

"Do Daryl and Maggie know yet?" She looks up hesitantly.

"About us?" I clarify, and she nods. "Not yet, no. But I'd really love to tell them. We could tell them together?"

Evan goes as white as snow. "No. I wouldn't want to do that."

"Okay, yeah, okay, of course," I say, jumbled as one long word. "Sorry," I add for good measure. "I'll tell them."

"Just... they might not respond like you think they will."

I sigh, unsure of what to say. I don't want to invalidate her fears, but I do want to reassure her. "Right. I can talk to them first."

"Okay." Evan nods, then scratches her chin. "Can I think about it?"

"Sure," I say, suddenly feeling shy. "Of course."

She notices. "It's not that I don't want to spend Christmas with you. I do."

I force a smile. "I know."

"It's a lot for me to consider going back there. It's been easier to tell myself I never would."

"I'll understand if you can't." I squeeze her hand tightly. "We can always ask my parents to come here next year."

Evan's subtle, warm smile appears like a sunrise coming up over a hill. "Next year, *huh*?"

I reach over her lap to hit Play on the remote. "You heard me," I say, snuggling into her side.

"Next year..." she sighs out contentedly, as if she can't quite believe it.

"Hush, he's proposing!"

She kisses the top of my head, and I decide that I *might* have to force her to come along after all. I hate the idea of not being around her for a minute, especially during my favourite time of year.

Sixteen

Evan

December 9th

The last seven days have flown by. A bit like a dream but more like a blur. We spent most of the weekend after the gallery opening in bed. On Monday, I took the kids on a field trip to a Christmas tree farm. There was one tiny, perfectly symmetrical, adorable tree by the exit that reminded me so much of Clara I had to have it.

It's now in my classroom, decorated to the max. And while I'm fairly certain it's against school policy to have a *real* tree, I couldn't help myself when my students begged for it to stay.

Clara went back to her place on Monday after work to convince her roommates that she hadn't been kidnapped. I went over there for dinner the next day after she told them about the evolution of our agreement. They grilled me a fair amount, but I understood why. I'm protective of Clara too. Altogether, it was a really nice evening.

Jen, Clara's roommate who seems to have some suppressed anger yet dresses like she teaches yoga made homemade shepherd's pie. Which, while delicious, is a bit of a sensory meltdown waiting to happen. Mushy potatoes stacked on top of soft, wet meat with vegetables in varying textures? Yikes. I still manage to eat it, distracted by pleasant conversation.

Leah, Clara's other roommate, brought out the board game *Catan* after dinner. We quickly formed an alliance to not trade with the others. She won, but it almost felt like I did because we were neck and neck throughout and trounced the others. I had a lot of fun, but I was most excited to have Clara back at my place and all to myself afterward. I'd missed her after just one night apart. I'd slept like shit without her next to me.

I get to have her with me for at least a few more days because tomorrow is the party at Natalie's. It's also my self-appointed deadline to give Clara an answer about going home for Christmas. I didn't want her to have to wait this long.

I know on a fundamental level that Daryl and Maggie are not like my parents. As a prime example, they took me in when mine kicked me out. But there are so many areas that intersect between their life and my family. The same small town. The same gossipy church. The same cycle of holiday traditions that most folks back home run through each year.

Pick up your tree from Ralph's farm, then sleigh rides and eggnog afterwards. On December twenty-third, Main Street holds their window-display contest. Then the Christmas Eve service at the church with hymns by candlelight. Followed by ice skating behind the high school on Christmas day.

I've told myself for ten years that I wouldn't go back. That I wouldn't get to do those things again. I'd successfully convinced myself I didn't *want* to do them. So now, it's really fucking difficult to convince myself otherwise. Even if it feels that Clara is the *only* reason to do anything.

She's totally not worried about that phone call to her parents. Not at all. I'm terrified that she's going to have a hard and fast lesson in the difference between your parents finding out your friend is gay and telling your parents *you* are gay.

Please let Daryl and Maggie stay cool.

I, of course, reserve my right to bail on the whole thing if they don't take the news kindly. Clara argued that it wouldn't be bailing in that case—because she wouldn't be going either. Still, it's good to have a proverbial parachute.

Today's been the perfect day to stew over my answer. I've asked my students to pair up, interview a teacher or staff member of their choice, and then create a presentation about them. So far, we've had three presentations about the office manager, Gladys, who is a fan favourite due to her candy stash. Another about the gym teacher, Mike, and one about the vice-principal that read more like a hit piece.

So, after hours of careful consideration, I'm leaning towards saying yes.

Every time I imagine Bagel and me sitting at home on Christmas day by ourselves, unwrapping a can of tuna and a pair of socks, I get sad. Not just because of the sorry excuse for gifts but because Clara should be with us too. *We* should be with Clara. I'm pretty much uninterested in any day that doesn't involve her from now on, but especially the important ones.

And though I'll see her tonight, I pull out my phone under my desk and sneak her a text.

EVAN: Tell Daryl and Maggie you'll be bringing two guests home for Christmas.

Her response is almost immediate.

CLARA: Really?!
EVAN: Yes. I'd be an idiot to spend the holidays away from you.
CLARA: I'm so happy! Thank you! <3

I type and delete *I love you* several times. "I'm glad" is what I land on instead. "Me too," I send before locking my phone away.

Seventeen

Clara

December 10th

Evan's fidgeting in the back of this taxi like she's about to shed her skin. I told her we absolutely didn't have to go tonight. Her colleagues would understand that she might not be comfortable attending a work party at her ex's house. Those two things separate? Awful. Combined? Positively dreadful.

But she insisted we go. So now we're two minutes away from a party that *officially* started ten minutes ago, dressed in green and red. My emerald two-piece suit, which is *adorable*, by the way, and her red dress. Motherfucking Christmas personified.

"Code word," I blurt out.

"Huh?" Evan doesn't turn from her view out the window as she bites the skin around her thumb.

"You say *persimmons*, and we get the fuck out of there, no questions asked."

"Can we think of a different word?"

"Russell Crowe."

Evan turns over her shoulder slowly, a smile almost present. "What?"

"It was the first thing that came into my head," I say, shrugging.

"Russell Crowe was the first thing that came into your head?"

"Yes."

She nods, grinning. "Okay... Maybe just crow?"

"That works."

Our ride slows to a stop, and the driver flicks on his hazard lights. "Thank you," I say, sliding out after Evan onto the sidewalk outside of the *annoyingly* charming brownstone. I reach for Evan's hand and wind my fingers through hers. "Hey," I say forcefully.

She turns, swallowing.

"You did nothing wrong. She's a jerk. Let's try to have fun."

Evan takes a deep breath, her nostrils flaring as she nods. "Yeah, okay."

I take a step closer, putting my chin on her shoulder, covered by her thick coat. "And I'm going to *very* much enjoy watching her realise how fucking gorgeous you look tonight." I give her bum a quick squeeze, and Evan rolls her eyes. "You crow, we leave." I kiss her cheek just as the door opens and Lisa comes barrelling out, laughing.

"Oh," she says, spotting us. She clears her throat. "Hi! Sorry, I was expecting Jodie—they're apparently out front but they must be lost." Lisa laughs weakly. "Um, come up! Come in. Please." She waves us up the front steps, and I smile sweetly as we approach.

"I'm Clara," I say, putting out my hand.

"Great to meet you."

"Evan's girlfriend," I emphasise, my smile faltering to a pointed line. The point being *fuck you, Lisa, and fuck your cheater of a girlfriend too*.

She looks so uneasy that I double down, wrapping my arm around Evan's shoulders. "See you inside!" I move us into a warm entryway, a pile of coats over a chair and shoes haphazardly tossed around.

Evan is fumbling with her jacket's buttons when a familiar voice wafts in from the other room. "Jo—" the name dies on her tongue as Natalie rounds the corner and sees us instead.

"This Jodie is so popular," I chime, tossing my coat aside with a flourish and fixing the lapel of my suit. "Hi. Natalie, right? I think we've met." I'm being a bitch, I know. She invited me to that party for Evan four years ago. I asked *her* what to bring. She welcomed me that night too. We talked about Evan, art, and teaching over vodka martinis. But that's when I liked her. That was before I loved Evan in this new way that has me puffing my chest out like some sort of wild animal.

"Yeah," she sighs. "Hi, Clara." Natalie looks right through me to Evan, who's flattening her dress with her hands. "Hey, Ev."

"Thanks for having us," Evan says flatly. "Nice place."

We stand there for several *torturous* seconds as they just look at each other blankly. I feel as if I could grow claws if I focused hard enough.

"Everyone's in here." Natalie turns and gestures for us to follow without looking back to make sure we are.

"Crow?" I ask quietly.

Evan shakes her head.

Two hours later, things are a bit more comfortable. Mostly because Lisa and Natalie have been avoiding our side of the room like the plague. I've met most of Evan's co-workers, and I'm fairly certain they all love me. I'm holding court with five of them when a glass is clinked, and all eyes turn towards Natalie.

"Clap once if you can hear me!" She laughs, and the crowd guffaws.

"Fucking hell," I murmur into my drink. Ev gives me a teasing *stop it* glance, and I take a long, thoughtful sip. *Minding my business.*

"I just wanted to say thank you all for coming. It's such a pleasure to be co-workers with you all, and we hope you have a wonderful holiday season. Keep drinking, eating, having fun." She waves around the room. "In a little while we're going to play white elephant, so I hope everyone remembered to bring a gift." She nods, getting thumbs-ups from several guests. "Great!"

"Oh!" Lisa pipes up, moving to stand next to Natalie. "Also, if anyone wants to join me for a quick," Lisa mimes smoking a joint, "I'll be on the back porch shortly." Lisa winks.

Nat looks at her with disgust. "Seriously?" She half-laughs, voice strained.

Oh my god. I grin into my glass—trying my best to hide it.

"We're all adults here, right?" Lisa smiles around at the room for reassurance but is met with blank stares.

I *should* feel sorry for them, but I love it. Call me messy, but I wish they'd start a screaming match right now.

"Wuh-oh! Trouble in paradise!" Jim, the other history teacher, calls out from the couch. A few people laugh, me being the loudest.

"Anyway, *we* are just so glad..." Natalie's voice fades from my focus when Evan leans in, her breath on my cheek.

"Crow," Ev whispers.

"Now?" I mouth.

"Russell Persimmons." She takes my hand and pulls me towards the hallway in the opposite direction of the front door.

Eighteen

Evan

Clara's struggling to keep up with my pace in her heels, but I can't slow down. I'm looking for a bathroom when I fling open a door in the hallway. I find a hall closet and decide that'll do.

It's a broom cupboard, totally dark, and not much room for Clara and me to stand without touching.

"Ev, what is happening? Are you okay? Why are we in the closet?" Clara snickers. "Ironic."

"It's the way she said *we*. Like... like..." My breath starts coming in uneven gasps, and I struggle to force the words out. Natalie was saying *we*, meaning *me* and *her,* just four months ago. It somehow went from *we are engaged* to *we don't work*, and something in her tone is leaning a lot more towards the first than the second regarding her and Lisa.

She seems happy.

Which is okay, right? Because so am I.

So why does it feel like an elephant is sitting on my chest?

"She's happy," I say, voice dejected.

"Natalie?"

"Yeah."

"She didn't seem all that happy to me. You heard Jim—trouble in paradise and whatnot."

"I don't know why that pisses me off."

"Because she fucked you over, Ev. She left you, out of the blue, after nine years and cheated on you. That hurts."

"Yeah, I guess." That's not it though. It was something about realising how quickly life can move on—how suddenly feelings can change—that sent me spiralling. Could Clara change her mind so easily? Could she go from *we are together* to *we don't work* just as fast as Natalie did?

"Do you..." Clara starts speaking, her voice hesitant and small. "Do you wish things were different? That you two were... *you know*?"

"That we were what?" I ask.

"Do you wish things were different?" Clara asks. I hear a shuffle of fabric, like perhaps she's adjusting her buttons. "That Natalie never left?"

The questions catch me off guard. Hypothetical questions are *usually* difficult for me to answer, but this one doesn't take me very long to answer. "No."

"You hesitated."

"Well, I was thinking that if Nat hadn't left me, I'd have probably married her."

"Right. Of course..." Clara's discouraged tone sends a warning jolt to my system.

Fix this. You can't lose Clara. You can't close up again.

I take a long moment, graciously granted by Clara's silent patience, to sort through my thoughts. One thing becomes clear above all else—I need to tell Clara the truth.

"Clara, I'd never in a million years have guessed that *this* feeling was possible. I'd have been content to stay with Natalie, never knowing better."

"What feeling?" she asks, an ounce of her usual hopeful lilt returning.

"That I'd spent my life as a half, and now I'm whole. Like I've been sleeping so long under a haze—an illusion of comfort—then you came in. Sunshine and golden rays of light. And you made everything brighter."

"*Oh.*" Clara's hands wrap around my waist in the dark.

"I don't wish I was still with Natalie. If this... me and you..." I stutter as she rubs small circles on my sides. "If I'd gotten a *glimpse* of how good life could be at any point over the last nine years, I'd have broken things off with Natalie. You have a place in my heart that no one else could ever have. I doubt anyone could come close."

"Ev..." Clara laughs, accompanied by a happy type of whine and a deep breath. "Evan, I love you."

I inhale sharply. "You do?"

"Yes. In all the ways," Clara says sweetly.

"All of them?" I ask. A soft, giddy laugh comes from both of us at the same time.

"I actually thought there were only two kinds of love before. That it was just love like your family or romantic love. But I think there may be hundreds of kinds. Love like a new lease on life. Love like a place to exist freely. Love like being understood. Love like the contented quiet. Love like freshly baked cookies. Love like a thin veil between wishing it'd started earlier and loving the way it began."

We press our foreheads together. All I can hear is the muffled party sounds from down the hall and our breath—heavy and in perfect synchronisation.

"Well, at least it's new for us both." I brush my lips over her nose in the dark. "I missed your mouth," I whisper.

"Just now or in general?" Clara asks, kissing the corner of my lips.

"Both," I whisper. "I'm sorry I freaked out. It's just weird being here. Nothing I can't handle, nothing that changes what we have. But it's still so strange."

"I can't imagine what that feels like, but I think you're doing a great job handling it."

"I'm sorry though."

"Don't be." Clara clears her throat. "But, maybe, did you have something else to say? Perhaps a reply?"

Oh my god. "Clara, I love you," I say in a rush. I cannot believe I forgot to say it back. I've said it so many times to her in my head, in deleted texts, and to her sleeping body that I didn't even think to reply out loud. "I love you," I repeat—just to be sure.

She sighs out as if she's been holding her breath. "Goodness, you really had me out on a ledge for a minute there."

"I'm so sorry," I say, bringing her closer.

Then we're kissing. A true, post-confession style kiss. All cards bared, holding nothing back. And it's a beautiful, messy, vulnerable, new, scary, exciting *thing*. Eliciting tiny shudders of anticipation up my spine and twinges in my hands as I reach for more of her to hold.

Her tongue slides against mine, and I hum into our kiss, opening for her. Clara matches the sound, her hand gripping my ass through my dress. I place two hands on either side of her neck, my fingertips scratching under her hairline. Eventually, my right hand slips down her jacket's lapel, tracing it loosely until I reach her breast. I pinch her nipple through the thin fabric of her blouse and pull my lips off hers to whisper, "Are you wearing a bra?"

"Nope." She pops the *p,* tracing kisses down my jaw to my throat, soliciting a gasp from me. "No panties either." She breathes into my neck. *Holy shit.*

I swear my vision blurs. We're in the dark, but still.

"Clara..." I whine like a spoiled child. Because each of the things I *desperately* want to do we *absolutely* cannot do here.

"Fuck me in this closet, Ev. Make me come. I'll be so quiet, I promise. I'll be so good for you."

"*Clara,*" I beg once more, but I'm admitting defeat the moment I hear a zipper. My legs nearly buckle when she takes my wrist and drags my open hand down her front.

"Feel." She turns my hand, curling it into the open front of her trousers, making me cup her pussy. "I can't go out there like this," she says in a small, sultry voice. "You and your damn words. Your sexy voice. I know for a fact that you're wearing stockings tonight and not your usual tights. How could I resist knowing that?"

She's soaked. Wet and warm and so damn tempting. I groan, pressing my head into the side of her neck.

She pulls me back straight with a tug of my hair to kiss me, and I'm officially a goner. Let it be known I *tried* not to do this.

"*Fuck it*," I whisper, gripping her like she's the side of the last life raft after a capsizing.

We're kissing so ferociously I wouldn't be surprised if one of us bleeds. Tongues and teeth and sucking and desperation. I push her against the shelving unit behind her with a thud and a clatter, a few items falling around us.

"Oh my god!" she exclaims, gyrating against my hand, searching for me to finish what she started.

There's no stopping this now, but we *do* have to be quiet. I reach into her hair, remove her scrunchie, and hold it in my fist balled up against her cheek. "Open your mouth." I push the scrunchie between her teeth, then rub her jaw with my thumb. "Good girl. Bite down."

She mumbles her agreement around the fabric, bright white teeth bared but barely visible in the dark.

With the sound being taken care of, I push two fingers into her. She was already so wet for me, I knew she could take it. "Keep quiet."

Clara's hands claw onto my shoulders for purchase as I fuck her with my fingers, deep and slow. Her whimpers come out steady and muffled, growing with every push and pull. I feel her tightening around me, her body trying to keep the pleasure from straying too far.

"There it is, Clara," I say softly, inhaling her floral shampoo. "There you go... That's it, Teens. Come for me," I whisper, flicking my wrist until she's grabbing on to me for dear life, her legs near giving away. I shush her, feeling her tremble against me. She moans her release out in a long, muzzled sequence that leaves her head hanging between us and her eyes squeezed shut.

When she eventually stands—finding her balance like Bambi on ice—I help her tie her hair back into a low ponytail and kiss her as she fixes her trousers.

Then, unsure of what to do, I use one of Natalie and Lisa's spare towels from the shelf to wipe my hand clean. It felt good, I'll admit it. A little final act of vengeance. But *only* because I'm ready to move on now. Ready to *never* look back.

Nineteen

Clara

December 23rd

The thirteen days between the dreaded holiday party that ended with a *bang* and a *bong* (no, really. Teachers smoke weed at these things—I haven't seen that many bong hits since college) went by in a dazzling, loved-up haze.

I'm getting used to waking up with Evan's alarms. I even got up with her one morning. Was it so she could make me coffee before I got back into bed? Yes. Did I also get kisses with it? Yes, I did.

I'm really enjoying being spoiled by her. Almost as much as I enjoy spoiling her back.

I'm also a big fan of staying at her apartment. It's less chaotic than mine. Though Jen and Leah are great, I doubt they miss my shower singing or kitchen experiments gone wrong all that much.

Also, Bagel has warmed to me. Well, sort of. He's tolerating me to the point where he lets me pour his food into the bowl without flipping it in an act of defiance. I warned my mother about him on our phone call last week, but I doubt she was fully paying attention, considering how the conversation started.

Hi! Just six days now. I've gotten all the decorations out of the attic. Don't worry, I left them for us to open together. Of course your father and I insist we stick to our yearly tradition of cutting down a tree at Ralph's. Also, I forgot to mention that your father and the Carmichaels aren't feuding anymore, so we can go to the ice rink behind the school on Christmas if you'd like. I know you used to love—

Mom, I'm gay.

Well, 'tis the season. Anyway, do you have skates?

No, Mom. I'm gay. A lesbian. Well, maybe more bisexual—because Henry Cavill and a few others but—

Oh!

And I'd like to bring my girlfriend home with me for Christmas if that's okay.

Oh, um, I'd say yes, but you know how your father is with meeting strangers.

Well, that's actually the best part...

It went well. She put me on speaker when my dad got back in from cutting firewood, and he took it just as well too. Though he was confused at first.

Honey, it's not a video call! She can't see your nodding—be approving out loud!

That's wonderful, Teens. Nice work.

Work? Daryl, she didn't get a promotion. Our daughter found love.

Why don't you just write down what you want me to say, and I'll say it, Maggie.

They fought for a few minutes while I made tea and tried to pet Bagel (who only hissed once!). Eventually, it was settled. Evan and Bagel were coming home for Christmas with me—and therefore my mother had to hang up our call expeditiously. She had shopping to do.

I, of course, relayed all of this to Evan later that evening. I think it settled her slightly, but I can still see the tension stirring below the surface. It's confirmed further by the anxious fidgeting she's been doing in the passenger seat since we set off for my parents' a few hours ago.

Evan's doing a brave thing, going home to a place that hasn't felt like home for a long time, if ever.

I never realised it before, but for *her*, this exile of sorts didn't start on her eighteenth birthday. She was harbouring that secret for so long, pushing it further down until it lived in her gut and sat like poison in her stomach. She knew the conversation had to happen eventually. She'd long expected what her parents' response was going to be. But she did it anyway. She gave them a truth they were not owed. Because Evan's fucking brave.

And while I wish she didn't have to be anymore, this is another courageous thing she's decided to do. To see the town, the familiar buildings, streets, and shops, where she felt so defeated.

Part of me has wondered if I shouldn't have asked her to come along, but most of me is glad I did. Not just because I get to spend the holidays with her, but because the angry, defensive woman I am would *love* to see her family start shit. I'm not afraid of them.

From now on, if I have any say in it, Evan will visit her hometown whenever she pleases. We have every right to be there. Everyone deserves to go home again.

My parents greet us on the front porch of the blue colonial home I grew up in. They got a lot more snow than we did in the city, but I can still see the familiar trim around the shutters of the main floor windows—the hearts carved out on each bottom corner. My favourite piece of the house is the dark oak door that doesn't match. My father claimed it would block out the cold better than any *cheap* storm door ever could.

He cut it a little too short. There's always a draft. My mother doesn't have the heart to tell him, but he must know.

They've got identical winter jackets this year, though I know they'd deny it if I pointed it out. *Most clothing is black, Clara, stop teasing.*

I honk the horn a few times, rapid and abrupt, as my father does the *old man jog* down the front steps and taps on the hood of our rental sedan. I check in on Evan over my shoulder. She's waving to my mother and unlatching her belt.

I open the door, climb out of the front seat, and hop into my dad's arms.

"Oh, Teens. Good ta see ya." His Newfie accent is always stronger when he's feeling particularly emotional.

"Hey, pops." I step back as his gloved hand reaches for my cheek.

"Luggage?" he asks.

"Yes, too much, as usual." I wink.

He blows out a breath, trilling his lips. "And now there's two of yas." He shakes his head, walking to the trunk.

I look around for Evan, searching the front and back seat, where Bagel is still sitting in his travel crate. But I don't spot her until I look back at the porch, where she's totally wrapped around my mom.

I do a silent count of *four Mississippis.* They don't part. My heart warms and pulses so rapidly it's as if it's trying to escape my chest and launch itself towards the two women I love most.

"She needed that hug," I say quietly, pushing my hip against my dad, who's about the same height as me. *Closer to the ground means easier work,* he always says.

"So did your ma. She's made a fuss for you girls. No complaints, yah? She never did forgive the Pauls for putting their daughter out."

I reach for the third of our suitcases, and my father pats my hand. "Let me."

"It's Evan's bag... let me."

"Ah, gotcha. Chivalry." His nose twitches, and his peppered moustache bounces.

"Exactly." I bite down my smile, shutting the trunk and following after him.

"Hi, remember me?" I ask, dropping Evan's suitcase down and attempting to get my mother's attention with outstretched arms.

"Oh, this is nice! I've never gotten to make you jealous without a sibling and all." She pats Evan's cheek before wrapping me up in a far-too-tight squeeze. "Missed you, darling."

My mother is perfectly plump. Therefore, her hugs are like heaven. I reactively shut my eyes tight, expecting a long embrace, but once we relax and sway side to side, I open my eyes to see Evan watching us, her wet, teary eyes filled with affection. Then they quickly turn to horror.

"Shit! We left Bagel!" She takes off running down the porch steps.

Twenty

Evan

The Spencer family has more traditions than I can count.

Shortly after we arrived, we put our things upstairs, forced Bagel out of his carrier, and got straight to the Christmas conventions. Which apparently start with welcome-home gifts on our bed. Matching pyjamas for us both, a Christmas mug each, a bottle of wine, toiletries, and some snacks. Maggie said she was excited to get the chance to buy more presents as we both watched Clara tear into a pack of chocolate snowmen from the doorway.

Seeing Clara in her childhood bedroom that we spent so much time in is beyond surreal. Because what once felt like a forbidden, silent wanting is now so vibrant, bright, and reciprocal. It's *my* Clara sitting on her old bed, biting a cookie-snowman's head off. It's *my* Clara's mom patting my back and watching her with a matching fondness to my own.

I've been informed the first item on today's agenda is to get a Christmas tree. And honestly, I'm nervous. While I know my mother is a firm believer in getting her tree the day after American Thanksgiving, I'm acutely aware that every time we go into town, there's a chance I will run into one or both of my parents.

And the image of that, the thought of the disdain and disappointment on their faces, creates a dread so thick that it lives in my throat like a wedge.

I play with the food on my plate as conversation happens around me. I'm half listening, half in a fog—my thoughts holding on to the house I grew up in only a twenty-three-minute walk from here, considered a neighbour by this town's metric.

"So we will finish up lunch then get going?" Maggie asks, clearing her own dish and walking it over to the sink.

The Spencer home hasn't changed at all since we were kids. Most of the walls are panelled, vinyl wood. A plate rack around the entire trim of the dining and living room combo serves as a home for many dusty knick-knacks. The same green floral furniture and one big leather recliner that Daryl fell asleep in often. The kitchen hasn't been changed since the house was built in the seventies. Old enough that the style is coming back into fashion.

"Sounds good to me. I'll get the truck warmed up." Daryl rubs his hands together before propelling himself off his dining chair with a grunt.

"Dad, don't." Clara waves for him to sit, mumbling over a mouth full of food.

"What?" He looks down at his daughter at the end of the table.

She gulps down a hefty bite of grilled cheese. "Don't start the car this early. It's bad for the environment."

"And it's bad for *my* environment if your ma gets cold." He flicks her nose gently, a great big grin on his face, and she swats at him.

"You okay?" Clara asks me, near whispering.

"Yeah." I force a smile, watching Daryl fix his coat and step outside.

"You sure you want to go?" she asks, her eyes narrowing on me.

"Yeah."

"Say the word and we leave, okay?"

"Yeah," I say from my trance-like state, focused on the salt and pepper shakers shaped like little mice.

"Evan..." I hear my name but don't look up.

Will my parents be there? Will they yell at me? Will they know they were right to kick me out? That I'd never change?

"Evan!" Clara snaps.

I literally shake myself, looking back at her. "Sorry."

"Please tell me what's going on in there." She pokes my forehead gently. "You look like you're about to start steaming out your ears."

"I'm okay, promise. Just a little tired."

"Do you want to just stay home? Unpack? Watch *The Bachelor* in my bed like old times?" She leans in close across the blue linoleum table. "Except *now* we can make up for lost time up there." She wiggles her eyebrows suggestively, smirk growing.

I'm grateful for the levity of her words, the way she can centre me like no one else can. "I guess I'm more nervous about running into my parents than I thought."

"I thought you might be. Mom knows the cars they drive. If we see them parked anywhere, we avoid it. If you want to leave, we come home. Everyone here is on team *fuck-the-Pauls.*"

"That doesn't include you, of course." Maggie winks at me, tying her scarf by the front door. "And I wanted it to be *deck-the-Pauls.*" She mimes punching the air. "I'm tougher than I look." Maggie's outside before Clara and I get the chance to laugh.

The smile Clara planted grows with Maggie's care. "You know, I think I prefer deck-the-Pauls."

"Oh but when *I* make puns, it's cringey." Clara throws her hands up exaggeratedly, smirking down at me. She lowers them, offering to pull me up and towards the door. "This is *your* town now, baby." She kisses my cheek, holding out my coat for me. "Ours," she whispers, planting her forehead to mine. "No one is going to mess with this. With us. Nobody."

I nod, kissing her just once. "What comes after the tree cutting?"

"My parents usually splurge on hot cocoa and spiked eggnog at Ralph's. Sometimes we indulge in a sleigh ride too."

I slip my hands into my gloves. "You mean the sleigh pulled by the old tractor?"

Clara gasps, clutching her chest with one hand that is still holding a limp mitten. "How dare you! His name is John-Rein-Deere!"

"Oy Vey." I tighten my scarf and realise that it's now just boots left to go, causing a spike of anxiety. "Clara?"

"Hmm?" She turns, fully dressed and half out the door.

"Thank you for bringing me here." I hesitate to continue. "I hope... I hope I'm not ruining any of this for you. I hope I don't ruin it."

"Never." She takes my hand and tugs me to her. "Impossible." She kisses me, soft and gentle and warm in contrast to the winter air spilling inside. "I love you, Evan Paul. I love being home, and I love Christmas with my parents, but not as much as I love you."

How'd I get so lucky?

"Enough of that guilty expression." She points to my face. "You've earned a happily ever after, and I hope that's me." She tugs my beanie down past my eyebrows, pushing my glasses down my nose.

I follow her to Daryl's truck, which is throbbing with the sound of "Feliz Navidad," even with all the windows shut tight. *She is most definitely my happily ever after.*

Twenty-One

Clara

Evan switched between shifting eyes, forced smiles, and lip-biting all afternoon. All through the tree selection and cutting. All through placing it in the back of the truck and the hilarity that was my just above five-foot father attempting to lift a five-foot tree into the back without help—because he stubbornly insisted he didn't need it. She didn't even crack a smile when the tractor pulling our sleigh made a noise *distinctly* like farting. Not even a smile when we spotted a family of deer across the field.

Evan doesn't owe me her enjoyment, and I know I should try to just have a good time regardless, but I can't help but feel dejected every time she glances over her shoulder.

She won't even hold my hand. She denies every attempt with little shakes of her head and a frown so subtle I'd miss it if I hadn't spent the better part of my life familiar with her face.

But now it's nearing sunset, and admittedly, a part of me is hoping that the dark makes her braver. Because we've still got our walk down Main Street tonight. Every year on the night before Christmas Eve, all the shops down Main Street host a window-display competition. The shop with the most votes gets a red ribbon and bragging rights.

That may not sound like a worthwhile prize, but this is a fairly boring town. These people get *competitive*. Friendships are lost and folks scorned over it each year. We usually stop for a hot pretzel and waltz up and down leisurely. My father has a habit of talking *loudly* about other shops down the way to stir up some drama. My mother brings a notepad and takes notes.

Evan's parents have *never* attended—consumerism being the root of evil and whatnot—so I'm hoping she relaxes a little.

"I've been dying for a pretzel all year," I exclaim from the back seat, looking at the back of Evan's head as she looks out the window.

"They must have pretzels in Toronto." My mother turns over her shoulder, teasing gleam intact. Her smile falters when her eyes trace from me to Evan. "Evan?"

"Hmm? Yeah?" Evan turns slowly, a polite smile spread across her face.

"Do they have pretzels in Toronto?"

"Uh, yes. I think so. I've seen them."

"Make sure she doesn't wait another full year, then." My mother points a thumb towards me, and Evan nods.

"I wait on purpose. None of them could ever taste like Patty's."

Evan's back to looking out the window. My mother and I exchange weary glances. She turns back to face the front and turns up the radio slightly. I take the cue.

"Ev?" I whisper, leaning over, placing my chin on her shoulder. "Do you want to go home?"

She turns, forcing me upright. "A little." Her nose twitches as if she's about to cry.

"Okay, that's okay." I let her fall into the crook of my neck.

"No... you love this. You waited all year for this pretzel," she whispers, nuzzling into me.

"My mom will bring me back a dozen pretzels if I ask. And honestly, I'm a little tired."

"No, you're not," she argues.

I'm not. "Dad?" My father reaches for the volume dial. "Could you drop us home? We're worried about Bagel being there alone."

"I think we've got time to turn around, check on him, and come back," he offers.

"No, that'll just confuse him. It's okay."

"But you love—"

My mother, as subtly as she can, reaches out and pats my dad's thigh. A silent signal that only comes with thirty-five years of marriage. *Let it be.*

Without another word, my father checks his blind spot and does a U-turn towards home.

"Ten minutes." I press a kiss on the top of Evan's head.

"Bagel's fine... he's in the back hall playing hide-n-seek with what I suspect is a mouse. My parents might not let him leave if he manages to catch one," I say, returning to my bedroom where Evan has gotten herself tucked in under the covers. She's wearing the pyjamas my mother picked out for us—red and green plaid bottoms with black shirts. Hers says *Nice*, and mine says *Naughty*.

Indelicately, I climb over her to the opposite side of my double bed, which is tucked against the wall. "How are you feeling?"

"Guilty." She pulls the blanket up to her chin.

"Well, I'd like that to stop." I brush her hair with my palm just once before she rolls over to face me.

"I shouldn't have come."

I sigh. "Why?"

Evan's wobbling lips catch me by surprise. "Because I'm ruining this, like I said. You deserve to be here, celebrating with your family and doing everything you want to do."

"I've had a *lot* of years to do things with my parents. Maybe it's time for some new traditions."

"No. You shouldn't lose them because—" She hiccups, a tear falling down her cheek. "Because I lost mine."

I *desperately* try to force down tears because this is not about me, but Evan crying is the saddest sight I've ever seen. I'd be a monster to look at her big brown eyes welling with tears and not let some of my own out. "They lost *you,* Evan. They lost out on knowing you. Their loss."

"Yeah, but... I..." She's struggling to catch her breath, so I help her sit up, rubbing small circles on her lower back. Bagel peeks his head around the door, hops onto the bed, and cuddles into her lap. I make a mental note to give him the world's best cat treat later.

"I lost too," she finally gets out.

I nod, trying to capture her wandering eyes. "Yes. You did."

"I'll... I'll never get this. I'll never get to sit in my old bedroom. Or," she stutters, wiping tears away, "or sing along to the radio with them, or—or meet my nieces."

My heart sinks. So she *does* know Michelle has kids. I wondered.

"Fuck!" she yells, startling us both. "I just—I'm so *mad,* Clara," she grits out. "I've spent so much time being mad. Mad at myself for not being able to change who I am. Mad at God for making me this way. Mad at my body for reacting to—" She stops, threading both hands through her hair, resting on her palms.

"I just wanted to be good enough for them. My whole life. That's all I wanted."

"I know, baby."

"And they *hate* me."

I open my mouth to disagree—but how can I? How can I argue that this, the pain she's felt, the way they denied her, is anything *close* to love? It isn't.

"They hate me," she says softly, resigned. "And I can't do anything about it." Her eyes turn cold, staring at the foot of the bed. "I think my mom knew," she says flatly. "I think she sensed it for a while. She was always pushing me away. Everything was surface level. Every chance to be alone, she passed on. It was like she was trying to bide time too.

"I always promised myself that I'd tell them before I was eighteen. That I wouldn't wait that long. So my birthday came, and it sort of... burst out of me." She wipes her chin. "They hadn't gotten to the last line of 'Happy Birthday' before I said, 'Mom, Dad, I'm gay. Please don't hate me.'" Evan's eyes find mine, a steadiness in her gaze that translates to rage. "The last words I said to my parents were *please don't hate me* and *please don't do this*."

"Ev..." I whisper, reaching for her cheek, rubbing tears away with my thumb. "I'm so sorry."

"And this fucking... hole... inside me. It's never going to close. I'll *always* be that kid who was thrown out."

I sigh, shuffling my legs up the mattress until my chin can rest on bent knees. "Maybe not. Maybe we could try and fix it."

"What? I can't see them Clara, I—"

"No, not that," I say firmly, then pause to compose myself.

"Their love, what they gave you before you told them, what they gave on their terms... it's not *real* love. It's not unconditional. It's not the type of love that parents ought to be prepared to give."

She swallows, and all the while the crease between her brows deepens. "Okay?"

"They'll *always* be the people who gave up on their daughter because of hate. But *you* can choose to not let that define you. You can choose to fully, unequivocally, unconditionally love yourself…. The way that I do. Maybe our love, combined, is enough to fill that space inside you." I boop her nose. "And the love of your friends." I tuck her hair behind her ear. "And your students." I trace her jaw with the backs of my fingers. "And my parents." Bagel meows loudly, making us both laugh. "Yes, and Bagel too…" I sigh, watching her take her first deep breath since we got here. "It could be enough."

She smiles, and it's bittersweet. A new spring of tears, a smile to catch them.

"Maybe?" I ask.

"Maybe."

"Worth a try?" I try to catch tears with kisses as they fall. Pecking her a bit like a chicken until she laughs.

"Definitely." She kisses the wrist of my hand on her cheek. "How do we start?"

"Well, I think we try to be… us… in public."

A deep breath, flaring her nostrils. "Okay."

"Nothing crazy…" I grin. "Maybe we just… hold hands?"

"Okay." She nods, her shoulders straightening.

"I'm proud of you, Evan."

"What? Stop—"

"No. I'm proud of you. I'm proud of you for telling them when you didn't have to. You didn't owe them that part of yourself, but you wanted to be honest. That's honourable. That's courageous.

I'm proud of you for building a life for yourself beyond them. For coming back here, knowing how much it might hurt." I tilt my head, forcing her to look at me. "And I'm proud to be yours."

A faint blush washes across her nose and cheeks. She wipes the last of her tears away and holds my gaze with affection. "I'm proud to be yours too."

We watch reruns of *The Bachelor* and fall asleep. That is until we're woken up by the sounds of my *very* patient mother parking the car out front and my *very* drunk father screaming the lyrics to "Wonderful Christmastime" by Paul McCartney.

Evan hums along next to my ear as I let sleep take me away once again.

Twenty-Two

Evan

December 24th

We woke up nice and slow this morning. Apparently, Daryl and Maggie's traditions usually account for Daryl having a bit too much to drink the night prior at the Main Street showcase. The hardware store won for their beautiful rendition of the nativity using only tools, lumber, and nails. Maggie's photos had too much glare from her flash against each window to actually make out what it looked like—which led to a long tutorial from Clara about using the lowlight settings on her phone.

Other than Clara's photography lesson, today has been relatively peaceful thus far. When we did eventually roll out of bed and saunter downstairs in our matching pyjamas, we found Maggie making french toast and Daryl untangling Christmas lights in his leather recliner. In a silent agreement sealed with a kiss, I sought to help Maggie with breakfast while Clara climbed up onto the arm of her father's chair and assisted him with one particularly nasty knot.

"I brought pretzels home for you girls," Maggie says, cutting a piece of french toast and dipping it in maple syrup. "Not sure how they'll be warmed up."

"Thank you," Clara says, warmly smiling across the table at her mother. God, she's stunning in the morning. Her hair is so messy. Probably because she moves so much in her sleep, as my battered limbs will agree. Not that I'm complaining. I just didn't think sleeping next to my dream girl would mean waking up to her elbow in my rib each night.

"We can always go back into town today… get a fresh one," I say between bites.

Clara bites down on a surprised smile, her eyes lighting up. "Oh we can, huh? Okay…" She shimmies side to side as she tosses a blueberry into her mouth.

Once we've all had seconds and tidied up, it's time to decorate the tree. Daryl hangs the star on top, adjusting several times so it's *just* right, and we all applaud his efforts. Apparently, they hang the star first, following a dramatic incident a few years prior, when Daryl fell *into* the tree and broke a few ornaments on his way down.

One by one, we hang ornaments, walking down memory lane as we do. Sweet handcrafted ones from most years of Clara's life. One is an homage to their family dog, who's long passed. Another is a very sweet but incredibly ugly crocheted heart ornament that Daryl bought Maggie when they started dating. They tell stories about his mullet and blue tux and her bright fuchsia dress at prom in 1983. Clara hums merrily to the music playing as she hangs a glass-blown ornament she tells me was from her trip to France during college.

Stories after stories are shared over the sounds of Bing Crosby and Frank Sinatra covering beloved holiday classics until the tree is full. Tacky and full and perfect.

"I almost forgot," Daryl says, stepping back to admire the tree with his wife. "We picked you girls up somethin' last night."

"Oh, early presents?" Clara asks over her shoulder. She moves one ornament up a branch, nods to herself, and then steps back to admire our work with her arm wrapped around my waist.

"It's perfect," I whisper quietly, just as Daryl returns to our side.

"Here ya go." He hands me a small plain brown box. "Nothin' fancy."

"Thank you." I smile up at him, unwinding from Clara to make quick work of opening it. I lift the lid off and push tissue paper aside, which reveals a small glass ornament in the shape of a heart. It is painted every colour of the rainbow and has our initials written delicately in white ink. And, as childish as it perhaps sounds, I'm so glad I get to be on the tree too. To feel more a part of this. Of this family, of this holiday, of Clara's history. I get misty-eyed before I even begin to thank them for such a kind gesture.

"It's an LG-BLT flag, I'm told." Daryl nods, beaming with pride.

"Oh my god," Clara mutters under her breath.

"It's beautiful," I say earnestly. "Thank you *so* much." I pass the box to Clara and throw my arms around Daryl, who's a good few inches shorter than I am. "Thank you," I say again, pulling away.

He pats my shoulder, looking sideways towards the tree. "Now to find a spot."

"Evan, you hang this one." Clara removes it delicately from the box and holds it out to me by its silver string.

"Wherever you'd like, dear," Maggie adds, coming to stand at her husband's side.

I put it right next to Maggie and Daryl's first ornament, looking at this beautiful tree of memories they've built themselves. Hoping this is just the beginning for Clara and me too.

The traditions for Christmas Eve, other than decorating the tree, are movie marathons and baking in between. Shortbreads, then Clara's pick—which was *Home Alone*. Candy cane brownies and Daryl's choice—*It's a Wonderful Life*. Red velvet cake pops and Maggie's selection—*A Christmas Story*. For me, jam pinwheels and *The Grinch*.

After hours of cuddling, too much sugar, and our collective fill of the Christmas Spirit—Maggie and Daryl got ready to head to the Church's hymnal service. They, kindly, didn't ask us to join.

Clara says she's alternated the last few years between going and staying home to watch *Love Actually*... her *actual* favourite that she refuses to watch in the vicinity of her parents due to its racier content.

We got about fifteen minutes into it before she was on my lap and my hands were under her shirt.

"I missed you," Clara says, kissing me at the top of the stairs.

"I've been here." I laugh, breathy against her lips as I lead her backwards towards her bedroom.

"But we haven't done this. Not since we got here." She plays with the hair over my shoulder, stringing kisses along my neck. We're stumbling into each other until the backs of her knees hit her bed, and she sits.

"Well, old house... thin walls," I say, shutting the door.

Clara shuffles back onto her mattress, then raises to her knees and removes her top and bra, tossing them aside carelessly. I have *every* intention of touching her, getting closer, revelling in each freckle and mark... but I don't move. Instead, I'm stunned by her beauty again.

The way the light is coming in, bouncing off the snow outside, casts her in a white glow. The angelic halo around her blond hair, from the same light. The crinkle of her nose, her cheeky expression she only wears when she wears nothing else.

"I love you," I whisper, not because I want to, but because I can't seem to find my voice at the moment.

She extends one arm out fully, reaching for me. "I love you too. Come here."

I take her hand, kiss her wrist, and place it on my shoulder. "How long do we have?" I rub my cheek against her arm.

"The service is at least an hour... Then they usually stay for tea, and my mother brought enough baked goods to feed an army—she won't want to leave without her tins."

"Perfect." I dive at her, making her giggle as she falls against the mattress.

Twenty-Three

Clara

"Clothes. Off," I stutter between panted breaths. "Now."

Evan laughs softly as she raises up from where she'd been kneeling next to the bed. Her entire mouth and chin glistening from my pleasure.

"I like when you do that naked." I attempt to explain my sudden demanding attitude as she strips off at the end of my bed. Her black lace bra and white cotton panties make my teeth grind together with desperation. I look up to the ceiling in need of relief, greeted by the posters I hung fourteen-odd years ago.

"Don't you *dare* look at Hilary Duff as I do this." A now fully nude Evan nips at my ankle, bringing my attention back to her.

"Look away, Hilary!" I wave at the ceiling. "My very hot girlfriend and I are about to do *very* un-Disney channel-like things."

Evan doesn't resume her position on her knees and instead crawls up between my parted thighs slowly, kissing her way up until her mouth is devouring the hollow space between my tits. "God, I love when you do that," I say, arching off the bed.

She smirks, sinking her teeth around my nipple. I moan from the flick of her tongue as she presses one hand down on my belly, curls it around my waist, and rolls us both.

Now on top, I lean down to kiss her. She lifts her thigh between mine and I do the same to her, feeling her warmth spread around me. We roll against each other, seeking out blissful friction. Breathing sharp inhales into each other's hair as we chase heaven at the same time.

"Sit up and turn around," Evan says sternly, breaking our kiss. "Straddle me."

I do as told. Whenever Evan is *this* forward, it always means we're about to try something new. And she's never steered us wrong. It's always so, so right.

She assists me in moving backwards until I'm straddling her with my knees on either side of her ribs.

"Sit down, gorgeous." She pulls me back, positioning me above her face.

Again, I do as I'm told, and I'm immediately met with the reward of her warm tongue against my entrance.

"*Ah.*" I gasp. "Yes," I sigh out, lowering farther.

Just as my eyes start to glaze over and close, being perfectly ruined and put back together in sequence, I see Evan's legs part wider, writhing against nothing.

I adjust slightly, giving myself a more comfortable position in which to start kissing my way down her abdomen towards my favourite piece of her. Favourite place in the world, really.

It's incredible how we fit together. I'm met with a dizzy rush, the blood flowing to the tip of my head as I bend to eat her out. The dizziness could also be from my excitement of having another new sensation and experience. One that feels *so* good. Giving and taking simultaneously. Control and submission. Power and pleasure.

We'll be doing *this* every night for eternity, if I have it my way.

Evan sucks my clit just as I curl my mouth around her. She hums her approval against me, sending a shockwave of pleasure up my spine. I show her how much I liked it by repeating in kind, reverberating against her. And then it's a pattern, taking turns to reward and receive with elongated, vibrating moans.

As pleasure crests, my legs start to shake, threatening to give out entirely. But this is a race I refuse to lose or quit early. So I play dirty. I pull back, admire the beautiful sight of my girlfriend spread bare for me—her sex swollen and perfect—and I pinch her clit between two fingers and start massaging forcefully.

Evan gasps, her mouth stopping and head dropping to the mattress. *I knew I could distract her.*

I tilt my hips up so she's no longer able to reach me. "That's it..." I tell her as she begins twitching under me. "Fuck... you're so pretty like this, baby. You need this? You need this release?"

"Clara..." she whines. "Please."

I stop the moment she says please and roll off her. *That'll give her something to whine about.*

"Leg on my shoulder, gorgeous," I say, positioning myself between her deliciously strong thighs. With one hand on top of her, I use my thumb to play with her clit. Slowly, not just because watching her lose patience is so damn fun, but also because I want the build towards her coming to be as glorious as the finish.

With my opposite hand, I trace the rest of her body up to her jaw as I continue working her. I grab her chin, tilting her to look at me. We make eye contact so intense my thumb subconsciously starts moving firmer against her.

I bite my lips at the sight of her. Hunger in her eyes like I've never seen, sweat in her bangs, and redness in her cheeks. "Suck," I say, pushing two fingers into her mouth.

She curls her tongue around them instantly.

"Good," I say, pulling the digits out with a pop.

I waste no time leaning back and pushing them inside of her, finding that same spot she introduced me to just weeks ago. She's whimpering now, and with every tap against her, each quickened rhythm on her clit, I watch her spin out of control.

"Let go, baby," I tell her softly. "I need to see you come. I need it. Please," I beg.

Her jaw tightens.

"Come on... let it go. Let it out. Scream for me, Evan. Tell this town who owns you. Who makes you feel this good. Please."

A raspy growl escapes her immediately. Her body tenses beyond belief. Then she's screaming out my name. A primal shout as she comes undone. I watch her shake and gasp and cry out for what seems like forever. Feel her tighten and tense around my hand, force her thighs apart when she tries to close them around me.

When she's finally spent, I lie down next to her, fold her into me, and stroke her hair until she relaxes fully in my arms.

"That was so incredible... It's *never* been like that for me." She sighs, kissing my collarbone. "Thank you."

"That was the sexiest thing I've ever seen." I twirl her hair around my finger. "Thank God we waited until my parents were out."

She laughs, the sound igniting my desire for her all over again.

"I think being here helped," she says, tilting to look at me. "Admittedly, I spent a lot of time in this room hoping and praying for just the *smallest* bit of what just happened." She smiles, shy and yet mischievous.

"Want to show me?" I ask in a whisper.

"Gladly."

Once Evan demonstrated her teenage fantasy—her being the big spoon, facing the TV, fingering me from behind as we both continued to watch as if nothing new was happening—we decided that we probably had enough time for a bath before my parents returned.

Soaking in glorious lavender bubbles, we talk about nothing and everything in perfect succession. The silly, the mundane, and the hopeful. The future we could write together, and the past we're rewriting. The memories we share and the ones we look forward to making. It's all so perfect. So content. So... simple.

Dare I say this could be my new favourite Christmas tradition.

Twenty-Four

Evan

December 25th

Apparently, there is one day a year on which Clara is a morning person. Not just a rise-and-shine at a normal hour person like the rest of us, but a six a.m.-present-demander. We, the adults, as Daryl labelled us, were dragged downstairs by Maggie and Clara in a fit of giggles. Bagel refused to leave his blanket mound at the foot of our bed.

Daryl made us coffee while those two got the living room *ready*. Meaning they placed each person's presents in a neat pile next to where they'll sit and located the Michael Bublé CD.

I believe Daryl made the wise choice to not offer my girlfriend caffeine, as she's quite literally vibrating with excitement.

When I sit, she flings herself into my lap, nearly spilling the coffee I placed on the side table. "Happy Christmas, baby." She kisses all over my face like a very enthusiastic, untrained puppy.

"Merry Christmas, gorgeous," I say, voice like gravel and eyes threatening to close.

"Drink up." She reaches over and presents me with my mug, still sitting crossways over me. "Good morning," she whispers, voice like bubbling champagne. "I love you." She giggles as I take a larger gulp. "You're the best."

"Teens." I laugh out her nickname. "I swear I just needed a moment to wake up. I'm almost with the living."

"Okay, good, because I may have gotten you a few too many presents." Maggie sits down in the chair next to my end of the couch as Daryl takes his usual spot in the recliner adjacent to her. "I love shopping." She shrugs as if to say, *it can't be helped,* and the simple, sweet gesture wakes me up just a little more.

I look around at these three people I love and feel an overwhelming sense of security. Suddenly, I realise that all I've wanted since leaving this town ten years ago was to feel wanted. Wanted for who I am, as I am. Welcomed with long hugs, cups of coffee, baked goods, and presents. They're not my blood, but this is my family. This was and will always be my home. This is where I belong.

And that's enough to stop all regret. All wishing things had been different. All secret hopes that my parents will take it all back and apologise. I don't need it. I just need to let myself enjoy what I do have.

"We go by age order in this house!" Daryl exclaims enthusiastically, reaching for the present on the top of his pile, and that's when I notice he's put on a Santa hat. "From your dearest." He brushes his moustache with his spare hand, making a kissing sound towards his wife.

"I want a fun hat," I whisper to Clara, who's playing with the zipper of my hoodie.

"Then open that one first." She uses her toe to push a present on my pile. "Saw my mom wrapping them. Matching hats."

Daryl opens a moustache comb from his wife and some wax that she picked up at a local market. He's very excited about this and takes it upon himself to use it while the rest of us open our gifts. Maggie opens a box with several sachets of Epsom salt soaks. Clara, a few months older than me, goes next. She gets a coffee table book about Kate Moss' modelling career, and I open my hat, which is green and has pointy ears coming out of it. It takes less than a few rounds of opening to realise that Clara and I are the elves to Daryl and Maggie's Mr. and Mrs. Clause.

We do this for hours. Open, talk, open, laugh, open, and admire. Maggie got Clara and me a lot of the same things. Practical luxuries like *slightly* fancier soap than I'd consider buying for my place, locally sourced chapsticks, hand-sewn headbands, chocolates, teas, and handmade mugs to put it in. I've run out of unique ways to say thank you, so I've just been holding Maggie's hand a lot. Squeezing her palm with my silent, overwhelming appreciation.

There were some gifts left under the tree that I deem to be the *special* ones. Mostly because Daryl tore into his brand-new fishing rod with the excitement of a man who knew exactly what he was about to open and had been waiting a while. He hands Maggie her gift bag, of the gifts she presumably did *not* buy herself for herself, and she shimmies with excitement.

"Oh... honey." She pulls out a *beautiful* wooden jewellery box. "Did you make this?" she asks, eyes welling with tears.

"Yes." Daryl beams with pride, his moustache bouncing with glee. "Look inside."

She unlatches the front of the box and gasps once it's opened. "Oh my."

"Let me see!" Clara strains her neck, leaning overtop of me, and gasps too.

"Well, now I have to—" I look over as Maggie pulls out the most gorgeous set of pearls. "Damn, Daryl," I mumble.

"He calls her *pearly*," Clara whispers in my ear as her parents enjoy their moment. "They began dating in June—I guess that's June's birthstone."

"Oh." I pout, leaning into her shoulder. "That's lovely."

"I'm next!" Clara says, interrupting the still moment in her usual enthusiastic way. I can't help but grin as she turns her back to me and dives under the tree. She opens a scarf from Maggie, handmade with all her favourite colours. Then my gift to her, which is perhaps not much after the pearl necklace moment we all just shared.

I rub two hands up and down my thighs, watching her delicately remove tissue paper from the bag I brought from home. "If you don't—"

"Hush," she says, winking at me, continuing to remove tissue paper.

"Wow, you really wrapped this thing," Daryl says.

"It's breakable…" I bite my lip, looking at Clara, who I believe, based on her slightly confused expression, has revealed the gift.

She removes the martini glass from the bag, a sweet but curious look in her eye.

"It's from the night we went out together. After your first day," I say shyly. "I, uh, after we made our agreement... to be each other's dates?"

"You stole this for me?" she asks, mouth opening wider.

"I guess?" I laugh. "I don't know what came over me, but when we were about to leave, I looked back at the table—saw the glass you used to toast our new... relationship... and I just couldn't leave it behind."

"Well, that's damn romantic." Maggie clutches her pearls *Literally.*

"It really is." Clara stands, glass in hand, walks over, and kisses me in front of her parents a *little* too long. "Thank you," she says, pulling away and sitting at my feet.

"Your turn, darlin'" Daryl passes two packages from under the tree, the last two standing. One from Maggie, and one from Clara.

I open Maggie's first, a box with tissue paper inside.

"This is more of a sentimental gift. I hope you don't mind." Maggie puts a hand on my knee and pats twice.

Inside is a small wooden frame with a picture of Clara and me at about six years old. Our faces are covered in chocolate, and we're laughing at the camera with our arms wrapped around each other.

"Aw, I don't think I've seen this one!"

"I remember this day..." I say softly. "The church summer fair—you and I were helping at the ice cream stand... It's how we met."

"There's something else underneath." Maggie pokes the box.

I lift out the frame and hand it to Clara, who smiles affectionately at the photo. Underneath is a DVD in a clear plastic case. I look up to Maggie for an explanation but notice that Daryl's ejecting the Michael Bublé CD from the DVD player and gesturing for me to join him.

I raise up slowly, slightly suspicious and nervous, before giggling as I hand him the disk.

"Why do I feel like I'm about to watch a *very* embarrassing home movie?" Clara asks.

"Because you are," Maggie says, turning her attention to the grainy video of Clara on the television.

Daryl hits play and takes his seat in the recliner, it squeaking under him as he lifts the leg rest.

Clara, same day as the photo but not covered in chocolate, is talking to her mother behind the camera.

"Teens, what are we doing today?"

"Fair!" a tiny, sweet voice returns.

"Having fun?"

"I am now."

"Oh yeah? Why's that?"

"I just met my new bestest friend."

"Well, that's very exciting... who?"

"Her name is Evangeline, but she likes going by just Evan."

"And where is *just* Evan?" Maggie asks, moving the camcorder around.

"Over there!" Clara points to me, sitting in the shade with a book. We laugh softly together, none of us removing our eyes from the screen. "She needed a break from people," Clara explains matter-of-factly.

"Well, I can't wait to meet her."

"You're gonna love her, Mama. I already do."

The recording ends with a fuzzy sound and squiggly lines.

I look between Clara and the television, speechless.

She's smiling at the video, almost in disbelief. "How did it take me twenty years to notice?"

"I coulda told you *long* ago," Maggie says stubbornly.

Clara stands, kisses her mom's cheek, and goes to fetch the video for safe keeping. I reach for and squeeze Maggie's hand yet again. Unsure where to even begin with all this gratitude inside me.

"Thank you," I say, swallowing.

"Last present," Clara sings, holding a long, narrow box. "Ms. Paul... you must *promise* not to ask how much this cost me."

"Oh lord," Daryl mutters.

"Promise?" she asks, eyes wide.

"Okay." I laugh, taking it from here. It's so light and such an odd shape that I have absolutely no clue what could be inside.

But the moment I tear into the packaging and open the end of the wrapped shipping box, I realise. "Oh my god!" I feel my jaw go slack as I *carefully* remove a long-stemmed rose from the box. A very, very realistic fake red rose signed by the one and only Chris Harrison, long-standing host of the Bachelor franchise.

"I couldn't resist." She clears her throat. "Evan… do you accept this rose?"

"What in the…" Daryl says, so quietly I almost miss it.

"Yes!" I jump to my feet. "Of course I do!" I'm giggling like a little kid as I twirl the fake flower between my fingers.

"Merry Christmas, Evan." She kisses my nose.

"Merry Christmas, Teens." I hug her, admiring the rose over her shoulder.

Best. Christmas. Ever.

Twenty-Five

Clara

We spent the rest of Christmas morning preparing for our mid-afternoon meal. Turkey, stuffing, potatoes, gravy—the whole lot. It was delicious. We pulled Christmas crackers, wore the silly paper hats, and told the bad jokes from inside them as we feasted. Afterward, it was time for the last of our many family traditions—one we haven't done in a few years: ice skating out behind the high school.

I checked with Evan a dozen times about whether she was absolutely positive she was up for going to a very busy town event. We'd most likely run into a few familiar faces, if not her parents. She assured me, each time more confident than the last, that she wasn't going to miss out on anything else.

While I'm quite literally a deer on ice, Evan is graceful. She holds us both upright as we skate around after my parents—who keep stopping for impromptu chats with fellow townies and almost causing traffic jams.

"Evan?" a voice calls out, and my stomach nearly falls out. But when I look towards the voice, I immediately recognise our high school English teacher, Ms. Jean. Evan balances me on the railing and skates over to say hello.

I take the opportunity to study the beautiful evening. The twinkling lights hanging above and the way they make the ice appear blue and green. The music playing from loudspeakers, soft and festive. The crowds of kids and parents and teenagers and old folks all enjoying this in kind. The magic of the holiday season bringing people together.

I wonder if maybe, someday, Evan and I will bring our kids here. I suppose we could adopt. Or figure out what science has to offer. I've not really ever considered it. Maybe Evan doesn't want kids. I know I want whatever she does. As soon as she does.

Because nothing in my life has ever felt as easy or right as this. That little version of me in my mother's home movie knew it. Evan is my best friend. You hold on to that person tightly. And now—she's so much more.

"Need a hand, darlin'?" my dad asks, pulling up beside me.

"Yes, please." I loop my arm through his, and off we go.

At first, we're quiet, taking in the ambiance and waving to Mom and her friends as we make laps. But then my father clears his throat, and I know he's about to say something he's rehearsing in his head. He's not a particularly quiet man, my father, but his cleared throat only means one of two things. I'm in trouble, or he's trying to say something right.

I don't see why I'd be in trouble.

"Teens... I gotta say... I'm so proud of the woman you've turned out to be." His lips rub together as he avoids eye contact with me, making his moustache shuffle side to side. "You've done very well for yourself."

"Thank you, Dad."

"And we love Evan, dearly too. Even her quirks."

I wince but smile all the same. "Well, her quirks are no different from mine. The more the merrier." We stop in front of Mom, who's ditched her friends and stands on the opposite side of the barrier.

"Two quirks in a pod." He elbows my side, smiling affectionately.

"The term is *queer*, Daryl." My mother rolls her eyes.

I can't deal with these two. "Go skate together, please." I shoo them away, laughing. "Go. Off with you."

I spot Evan through the crowd. She waves goodbye to our former teacher and starts walking back to the bench where she left her skates. Just then, a voice comes over the loudspeaker.

"Merry Christmas, everyone... hope you're still enjoying tonight's free skate under the stars, brought to you by Mavis' sporting goods. We are just approaching the end of the evening and would like to welcome all the couples to the rink for one last skate. Here to perform, 'What are you doing New Year's Eve' is..."

I stop listening as I watch Evan hesitate to do up her skates. I understand it's one thing to skate in front of all these people, in this small town, as a friend helping another friend balance. But it's a whole other thing to announce our couple status.

Focusing carefully on each step, I attempt to walk to the rink's exit without falling flat on my ass just as the song begins.

My skate slides out sideways, and I cling to the side for dear life as I begin to shuffle in even smaller movements, determined to make it out in one piece. Who thought putting razor blades on shoes was a good idea? Fully concentrating on the ice in front of me and nothing else, I make it to the exit and sigh a breath of relief.

That is until I look up and see Evan smirking at me. Skates on, stepping out onto the ice.

"Come on, baby." She takes my arm and places it through hers.

Speechlessly, I place one foot in front of the other. Clutching to her for dear life.

"Evan, people can see us."

"Yeah."

"They said *couples' skate.*"

She stops dead. *Oh, she didn't hear.* "You're right... we haven't actually clarified that, have we?"

"What?" I laugh, a stuttery manic thing.

"Well, we sort of transitioned from fake girlfriends to so much more without really discussing it."

"Oh." I narrow my eyes on her. "I guess?"

She pulls me to her front, arms around my waist. I look around the crowd—dreading seeing a familiar, disapproving face. But Evan's eyes are locked on me, so I give her my full attention. "Clara Spencer, Teens, love of my life... will you be my *real* girlfriend?"

I don't hesitate for a single second. "Absolutely, I will."

We kiss. Sweet and brief. But still, a very public kiss.

"Oh and..." I gesture to the music floating all around us. "What *are* you doing on New Year's Eve?" I ask. "Because... I sort of maybe told Jen and Leah I'd be moved out by then."

She laughs incredulously. "You what?"

"I told them I'd be moved out by the New Year." I wince, then attempt my best *look how cute I am, please don't be mad* smile. "Move in together?" I ask.

Evan's shaking her head, laughing more at my expense as she whispers, "*Absolutely*," against my lips. Bringing me into another perfect kiss. "We should get the fuck off this ice," she says, forehead pressed into mine.

"Yeah, it was a nice gesture, but I straight up hate this."

And, with nobody paying us mind at all, we exit the couples' skate and begin planning my official move into Evan's place. The start to our forever.

Epilogue

Evan

One Year Later

Under piles of discarded tissue paper, my girlfriend is giggling to herself. She just opened a gift from her dad, and I've yet to see what it is, but she seems awfully pleased with it.

"First your father decides to keep this gift a secret from me, and now I don't even get to watch you open it? C'mon, what is it?" Maggie rolls her eyes, looking to me for sympathy.

I smile at her, shrugging one shoulder. If I've learned anything about the dynamic of Clara's family in the past year, it's that Daryl and Clara like to team up against Maggie. Playfully, of course. But it seems as if this also means Maggie and I are becoming a team too. I like that.

Our team has baked goods.

Our team has also orchestrated a surprise for Clara that has made it near impossible for me to sit still all morning.

"Oh hush, woman. The rest of these gifts are surprises to me," Daryl says.

"Yes, because I do the shopping *every* year. I believe Oprah calls this *invisible labour.*"

"Dad, you should do the shopping next year," Clara says from the abyss of colourful wrapping she's buried herself under. She pokes her head out, a mischievous smile lighting up her whole perfect face. "I bet mom would *love* that." She blinks innocently, her voice soaked in sarcasm.

Maggie mutters under her breath. Something about everyone getting coal next year.

"So, what is it?" I pull *some* wrapping off Clara's lap in an attempt to see *some* part of her other than a floating head.

She holds up a white tube that looks an awful lot like spare plumbing parts. "I just have to put it together... it's an adult-sized walker for skating later. No more falling!" she chimes, holding up the instructions and narrowing her eyes at them. "Is this in Spanish?"

"I thought you said no to skating this year," I say. "Actually, I believe you said, *over my dead body.*"

Daryl coughs, a sputtering sort of dry noise that seems like cause for concern, or maybe attention seeking.

"Changed my mind." Clara blushes, exchanging a shy smile with her father.

Oh, I think. *Did I make it seem like she didn't want his gift?* Shit. I should apologise. Just as I open my mouth to do just that, Maggie stands and claps her hands together once.

"I'm going to pop into the other room to check on the *turkey*." Maggie winks at me as if she's never winked before in her life—her whole face twitches. "Just want to make sure the *turkey*... isn't dry."

Turkey was perhaps the wrong codeword.

I shuffle over towards Clara, collecting tissue paper as I go and folding it in my lap. "Hey," I whisper, "I think I misspoke. Did I upset your dad? He did that coughing thing, and you looked at him like maybe—"

"*Turkey* is all good!" Maggie sits, lowering a small emerald-green gift bag onto the floor beside her and hiding it from view.

I haven't seen it since we arrived here three days ago. I asked Maggie to hide it until we were done opening gifts on Christmas morning. I suppose that *is* now. *Is it hot in here? It feels hot in here.*

"No," Clara whispers back, smiling sweetly, "it's just... an inside joke dad and I have."

My face falls.

"Not about you or anything... just me and skating. I told him if I had a walker, I'd do it again." Clara's nose twitches—her body's signal that she's not being entirely truthful—but the way she's smiling at me and gently pleading with her eyes tells me to drop it. So I do.

"Okay," I kiss her cheek and shuffle towards Maggie. "Was that the last gift?" I ask, trying to remain stoic.

"Oh, shoot, I guess it was." Clara looks around, lifting a few pieces of garbage around her to double check.

"Well, in that case... Teens?" I stand and offer her my hand.

She sits up straighter, but her smile and head both tilt. "Yes?" She places her delicate wrist in my hand. I pull her up, and she lets out a bemused *hmm* from the back of her throat.

"I have another gift for you but... first... you have to get dressed to go outside."

"Okay..." She looks over my shoulder at her mother, but I don't take my eyes off her.

My beautiful girlfriend. My longest friend. The world's messiest roommate, as I've learned since last Christmas. My partner in all things. My (hopefully) soon-to-be fiancée.

I take a deep breath, a rewarding one that fills my lungs and settles me. This is Teens, my Teens. And I know she'll say yes.

I've picked up on the not-so-subtle hints. Gotten CC'd on several emails for wedding venues I didn't know we were wait-listed for. Witnessed the sighs filled with longing when the couple on *The Bachelor* gets engaged while she watches reruns with me.

She wants this as much as I do.

We all quickly head to the front hall and get our coats on. I sneak the ring box into my coat pocket while Clara laces her boots. Once outside, Daryl drags behind us, being pulled by Maggie and asking her, repeatedly and loudly, *what is happening?* She waves him off, wearing a shit-eating grin.

When we step around the side of their home, Clara gasps, then giggles, covering her mouth as she turns to me with eyes that scream, *this is about to happen, isn't it?*

Two snow-women greet us, complete with adorable button smiles, carrots for noses, hats, scarves, and sticks for hands. I made them last night when Maggie dragged Clara to visit her great aunt—at my request.

"I've been thinking a lot about all those snowmen I used to build in my front yard growing up," I say, watching my breath turn to mist in the cold air. "Every year, with each snowfall, I'd be outside for hours building them. You'd tell me the next day at school, or church, or wherever, that you saw them. And you'd talk about how much you looked forward to driving past my house. How much you loved them. So, I kept doing it." I pause for a breath, speaking faster than my lungs will allow.

"Sometimes, they melted before you saw them—but I still did it, regardless. Just for the chance that you would drive past, and maybe—*just maybe*—I could be a part of your day. Make you smile. Make you happy."

I run my hand over the velvet box in my pocket and get lost in Clara's bright blue eyes—already welling with tears. She looks between me and the snow-women as the cold turns her cheeks rosy pink.

"Clara, I'd like to spend the rest of my life finding stupid little ways to make you happy. I think that for you, I'd do anything. Nothing is too big or too small if it can make you smile. You're the brightest light in my life, my best friend, my confidant, my comfort—and the best stepmother Bagel could ask for."

That gets a soft, breathy laugh.

"So, Clara Spencer, Teens..." I go down to one knee, the snow instantly seeping in around through my pants. "Will you do me the honour of being my wife?"

Clara's nodding enthusiastically, and I *expect* the next words out of her mouth to be "*yes*," but she instead says, "Dad! Skate! Skate!"

I blink, searching her beaming expression for a clue as to what *that* means. Should I have asked his permission? Are we more traditional than I thought? But skates? Why would we need skates right now?

I turn and notice that Daryl's already running inside. Well, jogging. Mostly with his arms.

"Please hold." She looks down at me, smiling with all her teeth as a laugh escapes her.

"By all means. This is so comfortable." I join in her laughter, shaking my head at her. So full of surprises. Always.

Daryl shuts the door with a bang, and I hear his footfalls in the snow as he gets closer. He's breathing like he ran a marathon as he hands Clara her own little black box.

Oh.

"So Dad and I had this whole plan..." She wipes a tear, admiring the box in her hand. "I was going to ask you to marry me during the couples' skate... just like when you asked me to be yours *last* year." Clara lowers to the ground on one knee, mirroring my position.

"Evan..." She opens the box, and I get stuck looking at the most *beautiful* snowflake-shaped ring made up of purple amethysts. "You're my favourite person of all time, in all ways. I didn't know love could feel like this before you. Comfortable yet passionate, ecstatic but calm... you balance me out like no one else can. And I love you more every single day."

My knee is beginning to go numb, and I do not care.

"Evangeline, Evan, my everything, will you please marry me back?" Clara giggles. "Be my wife?"

"I asked first," I tease, biting down the smile that fights to take over my face.

She leans in to kiss me. "On the count of three?" she offers, inches from my lips. I nod, kissing her back. One kiss that blends into a second before a third tiny peck.

"Yes," we say in unison.

"Yes!" Daryl and Maggie shout into the frosty air.

"Yes!" Clara yells, tackling me onto the snowy ground.

I was wrong before. *This* is the best Christmas ever.

Acknowledgments

Thank you for reading Set the Record Straight! If you enjoyed it, please let me know with a review where purchased or online. I'm going to keep this short (just like the book) but here are all the people who kept this secret with me or read, edited, and improved this happy little novella of mine. Sophie, Tabitha, Stacy, Tarah, Ray, Millie, Esther, Lexi, Nellie, Laura, Kelsey, Megan, Crystal, and Katie. I love you all dearly. Thank you for letting me be your friend and allowing me to bother you with my content incessantly. Thank you to my husband, Ben, for being the most understanding after I said, "Hey, what if I put out *another* book this year?" Also, to our friends and family who watch our kids so I can write—Joy, Paul, Mary, Abi. Thank you!